ABOUT THE AUTHORS

Leslie Kelly has written dozens of books and novellas for Harlequin Blaze, Temptation and Harlequin HQN. Known for her sparkling dialogue, fun characters and steamy sensuality, she has been honored with numerous awards, including a National Reader's Choice Award, a Colorado Award of Excellence, a Golden Quill and an *RT Book Reviews* Career Achievement Award in Series Romance. Leslie has also been nominated four times for the highest award in romance fiction, the RWA RITA® Award. Leslie lives in Maryland with her own romantic hero, Bruce, and their daughters. Visit her online at www.lesliekelly.com or at her blog, www.plotmonkeys.com.

Joanne Rock is a three-time RITA® Award nominee and veteran of the Harlequin Blaze series. When she's not writing for Blaze or Harlequin Historical, Joanne is dreaming up YA books with her sister-in-law writing partner and fellow Harlequin author, Karen Rock. Joanne's books have been reprinted in twenty-seven countries and translated into twenty languages. She has a master's degree from the University of Louisville and is still coming to terms with sending her oldest son off to college this year. As the mother of three teenage boys, Joanne has perfected the arts of baking chocolate-chip cookies, removing grass stains from football pants and giving opinionated advice on writing brilliant essays for English class. Look for Joanne online at www.joannerock.com or at www.facebook.com/JoanneRockAuthor.

Karen Foley is an incurable romantic. When she's not working for the Department of Defense, she's writing sexy romances with strong heroes and happy endings. She lives in Massachusetts with her husband and two daughters, an overgrown puppy and two very spoiled cats. Karen enjoys hearing from her readers. You can find out more about her by visiting www.karenefoley.com.

Leslie Kelly

Joanne Rock, Karen Foley

A Soldier's Christmas

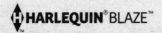

ISBN-13: 978-0-373-79780-6

A SOLDIER'S CHRISTMAS

Copyright © 2013 by Harlequin Books S.A.

The publisher acknowledges the copyright holder of the individual works as follows:

I'LL BE HOME FOR CHRISTMAS
Copyright © 2013 by Leslie Kelly

PRESENTS UNDER THE TREE
Copyright © 2013 by Joanne Rock

IF ONLY IN MY DREAMS
Copyright © 2013 by Karen Foley

Recycling programs for this product may not exist in your area.

Printed in U.S.A.

HARLEQUIN®
www.Harlequin.com

CONTENTS

LESLIE KELLY

I'LL BE HOME FOR CHRISTMAS

For Brenda.
I would never have made it without you.

_1_

Three Years Ago

"HAPPY NEW YEAR."

The shrill laughter and boisterous conversation at the crowded party should have made it impossible to notice even if a fire alarm went off, but Ellie Blake still had no trouble hearing those words, whispered by someone standing directly behind her.

Oh, yes, she most definitely heard.

What woman wouldn't immediately tune in to a sexy, throaty, male voice that seemed created solely for the purpose of saying _I want you?_ Especially when the pounding of her heart and the shocked pleasure racing through her said she recognized that voice. Worse—made her remember when that same voice had once said those very words to _her? I want you._

But no, it couldn't be. He wouldn't just come up to her and sound so casual, so normal. Not after everything.

"It's been a long time, Ellie," the man added.

Dear God, it was him.

She could no longer deny that she knew that voice. Knew it and reacted to it, her heart flipping and her stomach churning and her feet wanting to spin around so she could either throw herself in his arms or slap his handsome face.

Standing with her back to the dance floor, she'd been laughing with her friend and classmate Jessie over some of their typical New Year's resolutions—lose ten pounds, lay off the chocolate, stop spending money on shoes. Despite the crowd, she'd been minding her own business, feeling happy and content as she envisioned the coming year. And, of course, looking forward to the major changes the year would bring.

Now, all of a sudden *he* had shown up and kicked her whole steady world out from under her. Rafe Santori.

It was Rafe, of that she had no doubt. It had to be. Nobody else had ever sounded like that. Like heat. Like heaven. Like sin. Like strength. Like temptation.

Unfortunately, temptation was one thing Ellie Blake could not afford.

"El?"

She swallowed hard, watching as Jessie's eyes rounded to the size of dinner-plates as she saw the man who'd interrupted them. That was further confirmation of his identity. Rafe was the kind of guy women gaped at, with a face and body that were the perfect match for that sexy, throaty, I-want-you voice.

Taking a steadying breath and ordering her heart to go back into standby mode and quit the heart-attack-in-progress thing, she released her death grip on her friend. Jessie, apparently realizing this was the guy Ellie had talked about one sad, wine-filled evening, mumbled an excuse and scurried away. Ellie was left alone to deal with this hot blast from her past. Telling herself she was going to have to kill her best friend later, she glued a noncommittal smile on her face and bit into it, determined to keep it there if she had to bloody the insides of her cheeks.

Finally, when she felt as ready as one could to leap into a human volcano, she slowly turned around to face him.

"Hello, Rafe."

Wow. That had sounded so normal. So unaffected. So "I didn't cry over you for months when you finally said goobye, really I didn't."

"It really *is* you," he murmured as if he'd been uncertain. "In the flesh."

She shouldn't have mentioned flesh because it made her think of skin, which made her think of naked skin, which made her think of Rafe's naked skin.

Oh, Lord, allowing the words *Rafe* and *naked* to enter her brain at the same time was seriously dangerous. Like crossing the streams in *Ghostbusters,* the-end-of-all-things dangerous.

Especially now, when she realized he'd grown even more handsome since she'd last seen him. When he'd left Chicago to go to boot camp, he'd been a breezy, smiling, dark-haired Italian-American fresh out of college. His deep-set, thickly lashed, dreamy brown eyes had dominated his handsome face, though the sexy mouth had definitely drawn a woman's attention, as well. The body had been something to see, too—big, lean and hard. He'd maintained the build of the quarterback he'd been in high school, with a wiry masculinity and ease of movement that hinted he'd been racing wildfire on the football field.

But the past four years had made his handsome face even more handsome, if that were possible. He appeared more mature now, fully grown into his looks, that rugged jaw outlined with the faintest rasp of dark beard.

And oh, he was bigger. He no longer had a younger man's wiry leanness but was instead rock solid with thick arms, a powerful chest and broad shoulders. He'd always made her feel delicate, as he had at least six inches on her.

Now she felt positively petite beside him; he'd packed on a good thirty pounds of solid muscle.

Wow. She wished she had a cold drink in her hand because she definitely needed to cool off. Though, to be honest, even walking out of this club into the snowy Chicago night and dunking her head in a snowdrift probably wouldn't be enough.

"You haven't changed at all," he said.

"You have."

He shrugged, a small frown tugging his brow down over those dark eyes. "I guess I'm carrying a few more scars."

She hadn't even noticed the damn scars until he'd pointed them out. One was on the side of his neck just below his right ear, another barely visible beneath the stubble on his jaw. She wondered if that's why he'd gone with the whole unshaven look, to cover it up. As if a small scar could make the man anything less than mouth-watering? Good grief, adding the faint beard just made him that much more sexy; any woman would instantly be wondering how that sandpapery skin would feel brushing against the most sensitive parts of her body.

Some of her most sensitive parts woke up and did back flips to try to get her attention, ordering her to find out.

Not happening.

"You just look…older." Harder. Hotter. Sexier. "More mature." She tapped the tip of her finger on her lips and studied him more closely and admitted, "And a little weary."

Despite her determination to steel her emotions against Rafe, she couldn't stop her heart from twisting a little as she noted the faint, haunted quality in her eyes and the shadows beneath them. There was also a hint of gauntness in his cheeks. She wondered about the life he'd been leading that had both aged him into an even more spectacular man, but had also left its mark on him, a glimmer of sadness he couldn't disguise.

Rafe had been in Iraq for the past few years, she knew. Every time she saw a news story about soldiers being killed there, she went into a frenzy to find out the names, dreading the day she would recognize one. Thankfully, she never had.

He nodded. "*Weary.* That's probably a good word for it."

"Are you okay?" she asked, her voice low. She didn't want him to know how much she cared about the answer to that question. But she cared too much about the answer to not ask it.

"I'm fine. Really." He forced a smile. "I can't believe it's been over four years since I've seen you."

"Not quite," she said. "The video chats, remember?"

"Of course. But they hardly counted. I mean, they only made me more frustrated because I couldn't be with you in person."

She understood the frustration. She'd shared it.

Rafe had been her lover for such a brief time. It had indeed been four years ago, during the first semester of her senior year of college. She hadn't even started applying to vet schools yet. She'd been young and inexperienced, he a little older, cocky, with killer looks, an easy wit and a ton of confidence.

She hadn't understood what he'd seen in her, why he'd pursued her after a chance meeting at his cousin's restaurant. She'd figured it was simple chemistry. But the attraction, purely physical at first, had evolved into much more, at least on her part.

As for him? Well…whatever his feelings had been for her, they hadn't been as strong as his desire to go off to war. He'd joined the army, his goal to become a ranger. Before leaving, he'd told her that since his military obligation would last a minimum of eight years, he thought it best if they just remained friends. She should move on with her life and not wait for him.

She'd waited. Of course she'd waited.

But after a year, his letters had grown scarce, the video chats even more so. Until finally he'd said he didn't feel right about keeping the lines of communication open at all. She suspected he'd realized that even those tenuous strings had bound her to him, making it impossible for her to even look at another guy, much less give one a chance. And Ellie, knowing in her heart that he meant it, had done what he'd suggested and moved on.

So how rotten was it for Rafe to come back into her life now, of all times, when she'd just made a serious commitment to another man?

"Happy New Year."

"You said that," she replied.

"Are you going to say it back?"

"Sure," she mumbled.

He laughed softly. "You still didn't say it."

"Happy New Year, Rafe," she said, meaning it, hoping he had a lovely, wonderful, *safe* year—far away from her.

"You look great."

"Thank you."

Silence. What did one say in a moment like this? Other than, *What the hell are you doing here? Are you intentionally trying to mess up my life again?*

"No, not great," he said, that intense stare never leaving her face. "Beautiful."

"Don't," she whispered.

"Can't help it."

"Yes, you can. And you have to. It's been years, Rafe, you can't just stroll up to me at a party and act as though we saw each other last week."

"I'm sorry. I just…I guess I've thought about you so often, it feels like we did see each other last week."

He thought about her? As much as she thought about him? Damn him for saying that. For suggesting she might have made a mistake and given up too soon. For waiting to tell her until it was far too late.

"Would you like to dance?"

She shook her head.

"Come on, El," he said, and she knew he was asking for more than a dance. He wanted her to give him a chance. To do what, she wasn't sure. Nor was she going to let herself find out.

"I can't dance with you." She swallowed and stiffened her spine, staring directly into his eyes. She knew what she had to say, knew she had to nip this whole unexpected reunion in the bud before she made the mistake of doing something like dancing with him. Rafe Santori's arms might be the most wonderful place in the world…but she had no business being in them.

"Why not?"

A moment's hesitation. There would be no going back from this. But of course there was no other way to go.

"Because my fiancé should be here soon. He got called away on an emergency but I expect him any second."

His whole body stiffened and the small amount of color he had fell out of his face. She saw those dark eyes flash with emotion, saw him physically withdraw a half step, as if his feet had forced him to move away even before his mind had caught up with the new reality of this situation.

"You're engaged." His voice was toneless, his expression completely unemotional.

She nodded.

"Who is he?"

"Nobody you know. He's a vet." His brow furrowed, and she immediately clarified. "I mean a veterinarian."

"When did you…"

"We met last year and got engaged last month." It had been a happy day, and saying yes had been the right decision. She had believed it then, she believed it now.

But noting the shock and possible dismay on Rafe's face suddenly had her asking questions a newly engaged woman had no business asking. Like, *Why didn't you come back sooner? Why didn't you stay in touch? Why wasn't I enough...why was the army so much more important?*

Why did you come back into my life when I'd finally gotten over you?

"When's the happy day?"

"September."

"I see."

Rafe's whole body, already so tall and strong, went even straighter, and his jaw pushed out. He was putting up a wall, respecting her status, ready to back away. She wasn't surprised. Rafe's sense of honor had been one of the things she'd found most attractive about him.

"I suppose he wouldn't be happy if you were dancing with another man."

She replied without thinking. "He wouldn't mind. Denny is the most easygoing, laid-back person I've ever known."

Her fiancé was a good guy. A very good guy with a big heart, a great sense of humor and a genuine love for animals. Most of all, he was *here*. He was stable. He wasn't half a world away, putting up barriers between himself and anyone who loved him, refusing to allow anyone to get close...or to wait.

"Oh. So you just don't want to dance with me?"

"You mean the invitation's still open?"

"Of course."

A sigh escaped her mouth. "It's not that I wouldn't..."

"Ahh, I get it." The tiniest of smiles appeared on those lips. "You don't trust yourself, huh?"

"I see that ego of yours hasn't gotten any smaller."

"For old times' sake, Ellie," he said, lifting a hand and brushing the tips of his fingers across her cheek. "I've dreamed about having you in my arms again. Spent long, miserable nights clinging to that dream."

She closed her eyes and drew in a shaky breath. He dropped his hand, as if realizing he wasn't playing fair.

"Now that you're engaged, one dance is the only chance I'll ever have to make my dream come true. For auld lang syne, and all that. Whaddya say?"

She tried to resist, but that sexy voice, the need in his eyes and the hint of true emotion—as if he were mourning for something they'd had and lost—made her finally lower her guard.

One dance. One more time in Rafe's arms.

Then she'd put him out of her mind—and her heart— forever.

"All right, Rafe," she said, breathing the words out through closed lips. "For old times' sake, I'll dance with you."

HE SHOULD HAVE let it go. Should have let *her* go.

The minute Ellie Blake had told him she belonged to another man, Rafe should have swallowed his disappointment, ordered his heart to go back into the hibernation in which it had existed for the past few years and walked out of the party.

But he just couldn't do it.

He hadn't planned to seek her out during his holiday leave, which would end the day after tomorrow. His situation hadn't really changed. He had another four long years in the army, several of which would be in active combat. Iraq had been hell, but his next stop on his round-the-world tour of war zones, Afghanistan, was going to be even worse. So when his cousin's wife had told him she'd run into Ellie, he should have just ignored the information. Should have pretended Noelle hadn't mentioned Ellie was attending a New Year's Eve fundraiser for abused animals at a downtown Chicago hotel.

He just wished his cousin's wife had heard the tidbit about Ellie's engagement.

But it was too late to retreat now. *One and done.* He'd dance with her, build up the memory bank and then get out of here, spending the next two days with his family and returning Ellie Blake to the deepest corners of his mind and of his past.

He turned toward the dance floor, placing the tips of his fingers against the small of her back. Even through the shimmery fabric of her dress, he could feel the tiny protrusions of delicate bone, and couldn't help remembering how it had felt to drop his hand lower and cup the soft curves of her ass. Her whole body had always been so perfectly fitted for his, those curves driving him crazy whether she was wearing casual jeans or nothing at all.

The nothing at all was especially nice to remember.

God, he'd been crazy about her. Physically and emotionally. What kind of idiot had he been to let her slip away?

"I was wrong. You have changed a little," he told her.

"Oh?"

"You don't look like a co-ed anymore."

"I'm all grown up now. Eighteen months left of vet school, then I'll be out there doing what I've always dreamed of doing."

Saving living creatures. That's all she'd ever wanted to do. What a funny couple they'd made, considering he'd wanted to go off to fight and kill.

He pushed that out of his head, not wanting dark thoughts to intrude on what might be his very last moments with Ellie.

He looked down at her, staring intently, saving the vision for all the days to come when he'd have to rely only on memories to conjure her face. She was, indeed, all grown up. Her auburn hair was pulled back, a few long strands dangling around her pale, bare shoulders. He remembered scraping his lips across that collarbone, inhaling her sweet fragrance, and he couldn't take his eyes off her skin as they moved through the crowd.

He and Ellie hadn't been involved for long, just a couple of months, but she'd been the one woman he had never gotten out of his system. The sex had been explosive—they'd been insatiable for each other, and no woman he'd been with, before or since, had ever made him lose his mind and be willing to give up his very soul to have her.

It had been about more than sex, though. She'd been the first woman he'd really loved. Make that the *only* woman. She'd been his rock when they'd been together, and his steadying fantasy once he'd forced her away. He couldn't count the number of times the thought of her had calmed him in a moment so tense he'd been sure he'd snap.

And now, she really *was* out of his life. For good. Forever. No going back, no changing things, even though he wished he could erase that last conversation, when he'd told her he wouldn't be calling again.

He'd done his job all too well and she'd taken him at his word. That was probably the best thing for her. Unfortunately, acknowledging he should be happy for her, that she was better off, didn't stop his gut from churning or his muscles from clenching.

"Good band," she said.

"I guess. If you enjoy this kind of music."

He didn't, usually, preferring classic rock to the jazzy, blues-type stuff the musicians had been playing tonight. But he had to admit, this was a lot better to dance to…if the object of the dance was getting as close as possible to a woman who drove you crazy.

"I do," she said, turning to face him as soon as they reached the edges of the swaying crowd, though neither started to dance. "I guess I'm old-fashioned. Remember?

We went to that techno club one night and I ended up getting a migraine and we had to leave?"

He remembered. A smile tugged at his lips. "I believe that was because of the Long Island iced teas."

Her brow furrowed as she remembered. "Oh. Right."

She sounded sheepish and appeared embarrassed by the memory. Not to mention cute as hell.

"How many was it…six? Seven?"

"Four," she snapped. "They tasted just like regular iced tea."

"You were such an innocent."

"*You* weren't. You let me drink them."

"Sorry. I regretted it when I realized how sick you were."

"You regretted it more when I threw up on the way home."

He lifted a hand to her hair, unable to resist fingering one of those flaming strands. "I held your hair out of the way."

"Not one of my finest moments."

Maybe not. But what he most remembered about that night was how strangely good it had felt to take care of her. He'd never experienced that with a woman before, that desire to make sure she was safe and healthy.

That night, he'd made a resolution to never do anything to hurt her, if he could possibly avoid it. And stringing her along while he was in Iraq…that had hurt her, and would continue to hurt her. Which was why he'd forced himself to let her go.

"Well?" she said, holding her hands up. They'd been standing there talking as dancing couples moved around them.

He hesitated, aware that taking her in his arms would simply cement his certainty that he'd made the biggest mistake of his life in letting her go.

The song fell somewhere between slow and fast. And this wasn't the type of place for the arms-around-neck,

hands-on-butt, bodies-crammed-together type of movement he was used to from the old days, when he'd done
things like going to parties or clubs and finding a hot girl
to hook up with.

Christ, those days seemed to belong to somebody else's
mental scrapbook. They were so far removed from the life
he lived now.

Ellie, though? Ellie was connected to just about every
good thought he'd had during the long, lonely, dangerous
years he'd spent in a far-off land where everyone was either
friend or enemy and there was often no real way of telling
them apart until it was too damned late.

"I'm not the best dancer," she said, as if noticing his
hesitation and interpreting it as a lack of confidence in his
dancing ability. Not in his own sanity at having shoved
aside the one perfect relationship he'd ever had.

"You're talking to the king of two left feet, remember?"

"I suppose you must've gotten more nimble." Her smile
was faint, but there was a searching concern in her pretty
green eyes.

"I suppose."

Yeah, he'd done some dancing in Iraq. Considering it
seemed the entire country was mined, any soldier who
wasn't quick on his feet risked losing them.

He thrust off those thoughts. He only had the length of
one song to build up a lifetime of memories with the woman
he'd never been able to forget. And what he'd feel in those
moments seemed worth any lingering regrets later.

He drew her close, resting one hand on her hip, the other
twining with hers at their sides. They began to sway, and
he found it easier than he'd figured. Maybe because he
wasn't concentrating on his feet or even on the music. Only
on how it felt to finally be pressed against her soft body,
remembering the first time he'd made love to her, in his
crappy old apartment. They'd been insatiable, locked to-

gether, naked, hot and hungry…for hours. He'd buried himself inside her body, sure he'd never felt anything as good
as being wrapped tightly in all that heat. He'd lost himself
in her, and hadn't ever wanted to find his way back out.

Now, looking down into those eyes, into that sweet,
heart-shaped face, he lost himself again in those moments,
as if the past four ugly years hadn't even happened.

"I'm glad to see you, Ellie," he murmured, meaning it.
He couldn't regret finding her, even if it meant coming face-
to-face with the reality that he'd never be with her, that she
really had moved on and fallen in love with another man.
That she would wear someone else's ring and have someone else's babies.

Rings and babies hadn't been on his mind when he'd
left Chicago four years ago. War had. Fighting and adventure and adrenaline and patriotism. Living up to some
standard of manhood that Hollywood and boasting friends
said every guy should.

Tonight…holding her in his arms, knowing she'd never
be there again—he didn't think he would ever stop wondering if he'd made the wrong decision.

"I'm glad you're all right," she finally replied, her voice
soft, hesitating, as if she was unsure what to say. Maybe
she figured admitting she was glad to see him, too, would
have been disloyal to her fiancé.

Her *fiancé*. His stomach churned at the word and every
muscle in his body tensed.

He was envious of a man he'd never met, and would
never meet. Envious of the years that man would have with
Ellie, of the future they'd build. Jealous as hell of the nights
they'd sleep side by side and the mornings they'd wake up
bathed in sunlight as they listened for the little footsteps
of their children.

Around them, the voices of the crowd began to swell.
The announcer was saying something, the band had

segued from smooth jazz into a raucous celebration. He faintly heard someone calling off the numbers, counting down from ten. The revelers were ticking off another year, consigning to the past everything that had come before this particular minute in time.

He and Ellie stopped dancing, remaining very still in the middle of the floor, staring at each other. He saw so much in those aquamarine eyes—from love to anger to fear to longing—that part of him wished he'd left her alone, just walked away when she'd told him there was someone else.

"Happy New Year!"

Voices rang out, happy shouts, and the band began to play "Auld Lang Syne." All around them, couples stopped to kiss in the New Year, expressing hope for a wonderful, happy future.

This was the end of all he and Ellie had ever been and all they would ever be. He'd never see her again after tonight.

He had to say goodbye forever.

So without asking, without warning, he bent and brushed his lips across hers in a kiss as tender as it was fleeting. Then, his face close to hers, he whispered, "Happy New Year, Ellie. I wish you nothing but happiness."

Watching her through eyes that might have held the tiniest hint of moisture—though he'd deny it with his dying breath—he began to back away, melting into the throng. She watched him go, step by step, not lifting a hand to stop him, even though her tears said a part of her wanted to.

But it was too late. Far too late. You couldn't go back to the past. Couldn't recapture something that you'd intentionally let slip away.

All that was left for both of them to do was move on.

Without each other.

2

"ARE YOU TELLING ME there is not one single flight leaving from this city today?"

Ellie Blake stared at the clerk behind the airline counter, who appeared as exhausted and frazzled as the streams of irritated travelers swarming around her. People yelled from farther back in the line, angry travelers vented their frustrations on their cell phones, babies cried in strollers and fights seemed ready to break out at other stations.

Acknowledging this wasn't the woman's fault, Ellie tempered her disappointment and added, "I'm sorry, I realize you don't control the weather. But isn't it possible some airline is still getting out of here? Send me south, send me anywhere. I'll fly to Florida and change planes to get to Chicago by tomorrow."

Tomorrow. Christmas Eve.

She had to be home. Damn it, she just had to. She couldn't bear to miss the baby's first Christmas.

Plus Denny would be all smug because he'd warned her she shouldn't risk traveling so close to the holiday.

"I'm terribly sorry, ma'am. Every person here feels exactly the same way," the woman said. "But the winds are just too severe, and with blizzard conditions expected later tonight, all the airlines are canceling flights."

Why on earth did this have to happen now? Why did a major winter storm have to hit New York City the very day she was supposed to fly home to Chicago?

She should never have come here for the conference on new surgical trends for canines. She shouldn't have risked traveling right before the holidays with, not only Denny and Jessie, but also her sister, her parents and her friends also waiting for her back home. She'd never missed a Christmas in Chicago, not even when she'd left the country to volunteer at a wild animal preserve in Africa two years ago. She'd been gone almost an entire year, yet she'd still managed to be there with her family, drinking eggnog at midnight on Christmas Eve and waking up the next morning to an orgy of presents and goodwill.

"I wonder if I could catch a train?" she mused, speaking more to herself than to the airline clerk.

"The lines are already shut down. The tracks are freezing up; it's much too dangerous."

Ellie swiped a frustrated hand through her hair, knocking loose the ponytail that had begun to give her a headache. Actually, the whole afternoon had given her a headache. She'd arrived at the airport early this morning, having watched the weather reports and gotten the warnings that travel would be difficult today. Only to be told her flight had been canceled and the airport was going to close altogether within a couple of hours.

"I gave up my hotel room and there's no way I'll get another one. Great way to spend Christmas—on the floor of JFK."

"You'll have a lot of company," the woman said unhelpfully.

"I can't believe I'm not going to make it home for the baby's first Christmas," she whispered, imagining the disappointment she'd be sure to see in Denny's face and, of course, in Jessie's. The new parents had been planning for ten-month-old Annie's first holiday with all the fervor of elves training for sleigh duty, and as the child's godmother, she'd fully intended to spoil the baby rotten.

Funny that she should be so anxious not to disappoint her ex-fiancé and her best friend, who'd realized during Ellie's own engagement that they were far too attracted to each other. Ellie was sure they hadn't betrayed her; they both cared far too much about her for that. But she wasn't blind; she recognized serious attraction when she saw it. What Jessie had with Denny was something Ellie'd never shared with her fiancé.

And after Rafe had shocked her with that New Year's Eve visit, she hadn't been very successful at hiding the fact that she still cared far too much about her ex. It hadn't been fair to Denny to be angry about his obvious feelings for Jessie when Ellie had been a little less than subtle about her own for Rafe.

So she'd let Denny go, gracefully, calmly, and had been right there in the front pew when her ex-fiancé and best friend had gotten married the very same month Ellie and Denny had intended to say "I do."

The woman reached over and patted her hand, as if hearing the genuine misery in Ellie's voice. Or maybe it was the mention of a baby. Ellie didn't point out that it wasn't her own child's holiday she'd be missing; right now, she'd take whatever help she could get.

"Listen, you may not have any luck at this point, but a lot of people have gone to the car-rental counters hoping to get an SUV or something so they can drive out of the city ahead of the worst of the storm."

Hope blossomed in her chest. Yes, it was a long way from New York to Chicago. But if she got on the road within the next hour or so, she should, indeed, be able to get ahead of the storm. Driving through the night, she ought to be able to find clear roads all the way home and arrive by tomorrow afternoon at the latest.

It was worth a try, anyway.

"Thank you so much," she said, meaning it. "I'll go there right away." She glanced at the queue behind her, which had edged closer and closer as people pushed for their chance to hear the same bad news in person. "And good luck tonight. I hope you make it home to your family for Christmas."

Hurrying away, she followed the signs through the terminal, searching for the car-rental area. As she came down the escalator and saw it, she also saw that the lines were probably at least double what they were upstairs.

Hell.

There weren't enough SUVs in all of Manhattan to service this many people. Or even standard rental cars. Still, she wasn't going to give up yet.

Heading for the counter that she gauged to have the shortest line, she didn't notice that someone had stepped into her path. Not until she came within a step of walking right into a broad, camouflage-wearing chest.

"Ellie? Is it really you?"

That voice. Oh, God in heaven. Could this really be happening?

She looked up and saw The Face.

What did they say about déjà vu all over again? How many times in her life was she destined to run into this man at a moment and in a place where she least expected him?

It was Rafe. Older—pale, visibly exhausted—but still so handsome her heart forgot to beat and her brain cells began to leap and spark. He was dressed in rumpled fatigues and appeared unshaven, with eyes that were faintly bloodshot and a few fresh scars that immediately carved themselves into her soul.

"It is you."

"Hello, Rafe."

"I can't believe it."

"Ditto."

"Small world, huh?"

"Very."

"What are you doing here? You don't live in New York now, do you?"

She shook her head. "No, I was here for a conference. I was supposed to fly home this afternoon, but that didn't work out too well."

"Tell me about it."

"Are you stranded, too?"

"Yeah."

"I'm heading over to that rental counter to try to get a vehicle capable of getting me back to Chicago."

He glanced over and slowly began to shake his head. "I'm sorry, you're not going to have any luck."

She frowned. "How do you know that?"

"I just came from there. That was the last counter I tried…and they just rented me their very last vehicle. It wasn't even supposed to be rented in this weather, but the company apparently likes to help soldiers out, so they let me have it."

That was great for him. But not for her.

"I'm not sure if it's capable of getting me home for Christmas, but I'm damn sure going to give it my best shot."

Uncertain, she glanced up at him, hearing something in his voice, something that both excited and confused her.

An invitation, perhaps?

He made it clear. "Want a lift?"

She gulped, swallowing so hard her throat wobbled. "Are you serious?"

He nodded, that intense, dark-eyed gaze never leaving her face. Her heart twisted as she noted the circles beneath those eyes, the almost bony leanness of his cheeks, the stubble, the scars, the…the sadness. There was no other word for it.

If Rafe had appeared weary the last time she'd seen him, after he'd been in the military for four years, now, after seven, he seemed almost broken. As if he'd been to the edge of the world, witnessed the worst it had to offer and only barely managed to crawl his way back toward sanity and civilization.

Of course, she wasn't entirely sure you could call the day before Christmas Eve at a snowed-in airport either sane or civilized. Still, it had to be better than where he'd been living.

Outwardly, she maintained her poise, but deep inside, she wept for him, for what he'd seen and what he'd done and what he'd missed.

What *they'd* missed.

Damn it, how could he always affect her this way?

"What do you say, El?" he asked.

"You're seriously going to drive all the way to Chicago?"

A faint grin widened that sexy mouth, but it didn't seem entirely natural, as if he wasn't used to smiling much anymore. "I haven't been home for Christmas in three years—since the last we ran into each other. I promised my folks I'd be there this Christmas, and I intend to keep that promise."

He shifted his heavy pack from one powerful shoulder to the other, and she couldn't help appreciating the way the soft fabric of his fatigues hugged every ridge of muscle, from flexing arms down to thick, strong legs. He might be tired and careworn, but oh, God, was he still hot. The most masculine man she'd ever seen in her life.

This is not a good idea.

Being closed up in a car with him as they drove halfway across the country? It could take a whole day to reach their destination, and that was if they were lucky and got ahead of the worst weather. And every minute of the trip, she'd be trapped in a confined space with the one man she'd never been able to forget—the one whose very memory had cost her so much and had made her so drastically alter her plans for her life.

Could she really put herself through it?

"Come on, El. I could use the second pair of eyes, not to mention the company to keep me awake. Coffee might not cut it. I've been traveling for almost forty hours."

"Couldn't get them to fly you those last three, huh?"

"Don't I wish. Military transport got me all the way from Kabul. I never imagined a bunch of damned snow-flakes would stop me from getting the last eight hundred miles home."

"Me, neither."

"So, are you in?"

Another pause, another second to realize she would be making a huge mistake. But then there was one more thing. One more crazy thought whizzing through her head.

Maybe this was, instead, the luckiest moment of her life. It could be the chance she'd been waiting for...the one she'd feared she'd never have again.

The chance to discover if, after all these years, after time and distance and other relationships, she and Rafe Santori really were meant to be together after all.

She'd have to protect her heart from making the same old mistakes. She couldn't let her guard down right away. For all she knew, he had moved on, had totally forgotten about her. Maybe he'd even changed and was no longer the tender, noble man she'd once loved. War could certainly alter people. So it wouldn't do to let him get too close, too quickly. She had to keep up some walls, had to be cautious and go slowly. Mostly she had to avoid falling hard and fast and irrevocably in love with the man again.

Until she figured out whether she could trust her feelings for him, her heart was under lock and key. And the future remained as uncertain and elusive as it had since the day they'd said goodbye all those years ago when he'd gone off to war.

But for the first time since that New Year's Eve three years ago, she began to feel something that resembled hope. Hope for a future she'd been absolutely certain was forever lost to her.

"Okay, Rafe," she finally said. "I'm in."

RAFE WASN'T SURE what he had been thinking to offer Ellie a ride to Chicago. He'd never been a masochist, never enjoyed testing himself with pain the way some of his fellow soldiers did. So why on earth would he inflict emotional torture on himself for a good eighteen hours? Because sitting in this small car—they called it a subcompact, but considering the way it skidded and slid all over the damned highway, it should have been called a sleigh—with her for eight hundred miles was sure to be torturous.

You can't abandon her in an airport so far from home. Not on Christmas.

Maybe not. But did he really have to suggest she ride with him? The last time he'd seen her, Ellie had been engaged and happy, planning her September wedding with her nice-guy fiancé. Rafe had spent the past three years picturing her at that wedding, dressed in white lace, smiling and joyous. He'd tormented himself with mental images of her and her perfect, nice husband. Had mentally seen her painting their house in the burbs, adding a nursery when she became round and pregnant.

He had kicked himself whenever he let his imagination go down that road. But in the darkest nights, when he was bone tired and missing life in the States so bad he swore he'd go crazy if he had to inhale another mouthful of sand, she was all he thought about.

Conjuring up a vision of Ellie always brought him coolness, quiet, comfort. Which was really funny, considering he'd always been so hot for her. Like, seriously, couldn't-keep-his-hands-off-her hot for her, when they had first gotten together.

He still was. Of that, there was no doubt. Just sitting in the car with her, hearing her tiny gasps whenever they hit a particularly icy patch of road, or her soft sighs when they found a smooth stretch, was agony. Watching the dashboard lights play across her beautiful face, physically pained him. He wanted her so badly he would be willing to drive the rental into the nearest snow bank if only he could pull her over onto his lap and kiss her until the taste and feel of her mouth were imprinted on every cell of memory he owned.

She was lovelier than ever, if that was even possible. Marriage apparently agreed with her. Gone was the girlish roundness to her face. Those blue-green eyes seemed bigger than before, her lush mouth more mature and so much more alluring. Her body was all curve and slope, begging for a man's hands and mouth. *His* hands and mouth.

No. She's off-limits.

He might have done some things he wasn't proud of in his life, but he had his own code. And stealing another man's wife was strictly forbidden.

"It's going to be a very long night, isn't it?" she mumbled as he spotted a patch of black ice just a second before it was too late to ease off the gas to avoid fishtailing all over the road. *Get your head in the damn game, man.*

"Yeah." He sighed heavily, reaching for the foam coffee cup in the holder next to his seat. The coffee was cold; they'd grabbed it on the way out of the airport. Since then, they'd driven for four hours but hadn't even made it out of New Jersey. At this rate, the bloody blizzard would be ahead of them by the time they got to Pennsylvania.

"I'd be happy to drive. I don't imagine you've had much snow-driving experience lately."

"You might be surprised."

"But you've been in Afghanistan, haven't you?"

"It gets cold as hell in some parts of the country in the winter. And hotter than Satan's frying pan in the summer."

She shuddered in distaste. "I can't wait for you to get out of there for good."

Finally a subject he could smile about. "It's done."

"What?"

"That's why I'm so anxious to get home to Chicago. My Christmas present is telling the family that I've finally rotated out of active duty. My last year in the rangers will be spent training recruits, stateside."

God knew he'd earned it. His visits home over the past seven years had been few and far between, every rotation out of a hot zone quickly rescinded when violence flared up again. But this time, it was official, signed and sealed. He was to report to Benning after the first of the year. One year in Georgia, then he'd be free to return to his real life.

What his real life was, he had no idea. He just knew it would include home and family. Maybe not the one he'd once dreamed of having, considering the woman beside him was married to another man. But he couldn't deny he was looking forward to being a Santori again, rather than a captain in the rangers.

"I can't believe it. I'm so happy for you…and for your family. This will be the best Christmas present your parents could have asked for."

"It's the best one I've ever gotten, believe me."

"I see them sometimes, you know."

"My parents?" He glanced over, surprised. Although they'd only been together a few months, he'd brought her around the clan enough to show them she'd really meant something to him. Funny that none of his family's letters or emails had hinted that they'd seen her.

Maybe because the family was big on fidelity. She was

a married woman now. He needed to keep reminding himself of that.

It could also be because all anybody wanted to talk about lately was the fact that Leo was going to be a father. His kid brother apparently had a new fiancée and a baby on the way. Their mother might be big on marriage and fidelity, but she was out of her mind with excitement over being a grandmother. She wasn't complaining one bit about the fact that Leo hadn't yet wed this Madison woman he'd met just a few months ago.

Leo, married. And a father. He had a hard time imagining it. Of course, considering Leo'd had a near miss when he'd almost married a barracuda last year, Rafe could only imagine he was going to love Madison…if only because she wasn't Leo's ex.

"My place isn't far from your cousin Tony's restaurant," Ellie was saying. "I get carryout from there all the time."

Son of a bitch. And Tony had never said a word.

"You and your…husband, do you go in there a lot?"

She opened her mouth to answer, but before she could say anything, the tires hit a slick spot and the car began to slide.

"Damn it," he snarled. Gripping the wheel in his clenched hands, he steered into the skid, not fighting it and not braking, knowing that would send them spinning wildly. The road might be nearly deserted, but the guardrails wouldn't do much to keep them from going down a steep embankment on one side if they drifted too close to it.

He managed to get the skid under control and eased the car back into what he figured was his lane. It was nearly impossible to make out the yellow dividing line. The snow was coming down so hard the plows and salt trucks just couldn't keep up.

"This isn't going to work," he told her, cursing himself for bringing her out here in weather this bad. Jesus, he could get them both killed if he kept on. It was crazy to keep driving. "Maybe we should pull off."

"And go where?"

He'd seen signs for a town called Columbia, and an information billboard indicated there were some hotels at the next exit, which should be coming up within a few miles. "Let's see if we can get a room...." He cleared his throat. "I mean, a *couple* of rooms for the night. We'll try again in the morning after the plows have done a better job."

"Aren't we going to be following the worst of the storm then, rather than staying ahead of it?"

"We're going to be stuck on the highway if we don't stop," he said. And while the gas tank was still half-full, no way did he want to spend an entire night out here, stranded, with the gas slowly running out and the heat going right along with it. "I'm really sorry, Ellie. I guess this wasn't a great idea."

She reached over and squeezed his leg, just above the knee. The touch shocked him and sent heat rushing through his entire body. It was all he could do not to flinch hard enough to send the car into another skid.

"It's okay," she murmured. "I trust your judgment. Let's get off the road, Rafe. We'll get up as soon as it's daylight and make up a lot of time."

Right. Early in the morning, which was about eight hours from now. They just had to find a room—*two rooms*—and get through one night together.

He'd spent seven years in one violent, death-filled pit after another. Surely he could spend one night with the woman he'd once loved beyond reason, who was now lost to him.

One night. And in the morning everything would be much more clear...from the roads to his own head.

3

THEY HAD NO LUCK finding a room in Columbia. Everybody else had apparently gotten off the highway, taking up all the available hotel space. Ellie would bet half the people at these places were the ones who'd rented cars at JFK and hurried out of the city ahead of them.

Although all the restaurants and drive-throughs were closed because of the storm, a clerk at a small hotel where they'd struck out on a room had let them refill their coffee cups. The middle-aged woman had spied Rafe, so sexy and heroic-looking in his fatigues, and almost burst into tears because she hadn't been able to accommodate a "real American hero." They'd promised her the coffee would be enough and resumed their room hunt, both of them already doubting things would be much different at any of the nearby places.

"Okay, it appears we're going to have to white-knuckle this a little longer," he told her as they got back in the car after striking out at their last motel option in Columbia—a place that had seemed more likely to rent by the hour to locals than to overnight out-of-town travelers. Not that she would have complained if they'd had a vacancy. "Strouds-burg is a pretty big place. We'll get out of Jersey and try there, okay?"

She nodded, growing more tense as he steered the small car up the exit ramp, which had at least two inches of untouched snow on it. Fortunately, though, as they reached the actual highway, they saw a plow proceed slowly ahead of them, spitting road salt in its wake.

"Follow that truck!" she said, quickly pointing as relief washed over her.

"Done."

With the New Jersey truck clearing the way, they traveled deeper into the night and closer to home. The combination of freshly brewed hot coffee and the plow truck made the next few hours of their drive a whole lot more pleasant than the last few had been. They didn't exactly set any speed records, but they definitely put some miles behind them, even after they lost the benefit of the New Jersey truck when they crossed the state line into Pennsylvania. They didn't have an escort in this state, but they hadn't missed one by long, because things remained pretty clear.

That was fortunate, considering they weren't any luckier finding a room in Stroudsburg than they'd been in Columbia. They got off at the next two consecutive exits, asked at every establishment, and continued to hear there was no room. But at least they again got fresh coffee and more gas before they got back on the highway.

Luckily, the snow had lightened up a little. It now fell in large plops rather than nonstop plinks against the windshield. The wipers were actually managing to keep up. Ellie wasn't quite as afraid they were taking their lives into their hands by plodding on.

But that left her with too much time to study Rafe's profile, to recall how that mouth had felt against various parts of her anatomy and to realize that she'd made a big mistake by dropping her hand onto his leg. Before that, she'd been doing a pretty good job of telling herself she could

resist him and keep up her emotional walls until they got
to know each other again.

Now that she'd touched that muscular thigh, though, she
couldn't stop imagining tearing his clothes off and touching every inch of that amazing body.

Think of something else!

"So, where will you be stationed during this next year?"
she asked when the roads seemed clear enough to risk a
little neutral conversation.

"Fort Benning, Georgia."

"Georgia, huh?"

"Yep."

"Do they even allow Chicago Italian boys in Georgia?"

"Guess I'm going to find out in a couple of weeks."

"And what about after that? After Georgia?"

"After that, I'll be in the reserves, but considering the
amount of front-line duty I've pulled, that should be okay.
I'll be free to move home and pick up the pieces of my life."

"Do you have any idea what you want to do?"

He hesitated.

"Come on, you can tell me."

"You'll think it's crazy."

"No, I swear, I won't."

He waited a little longer before finally admitting, "I'm
actually considering teaching in an inner-city high school."

Of all the things she'd expected him to say—private
security, cop, bodyguard—high school teacher had never
occurred to her. Her mind was truly boggled. "Are you
serious?"

"Yeah. My degree's in mathematics. I could take enough
courses to get my teaching certificate in about a year."

"Wow," she said, still mentally reeling.

"I've experienced enough of the world to realize that
American kids are falling behind in math and science. I

want to get high school kids into learning. I think I'd be pretty good at it."

"I have no doubt you'd be good at it," she said, meaning it wholeheartedly.

No, she'd never imagined such a life for him. And no, most people who saw him in those fatigues, with that haunted look in his eyes wouldn't be able to picture it, either. But now that he'd said it, she could. She really could.

Rafe had been soaked in blood and violence for many years. He'd seen the worst humanity had to offer. So it made perfect sense to her that he would want to change gears completely, to try to make a difference. Why wouldn't he long to be around young people who hadn't yet been completely jaded by life? Why shouldn't he set an example—help them stay on a path toward learning rather than fall helplessly into the gang culture that so gripped Chicago? She couldn't imagine many teenagers having the balls to mouth off to him, and instead could easily envision them respecting him.

He could change lives. Of that she had no doubt.

"You think it sounds crazy?"

"No," she said, hearing her own vehemence. "It sounds absolutely wonderful."

"Thank you," he murmured. "I'll remember you said that the first time some punk slashes my tires when I fail him."

"I'll remind you I said it the first time a valedictorian thanks you for helping him get into Stanford."

"You've got a deal."

She suspected he might experience both kinds of students if he taught in some of the neediest schools, but she also suspected that was exactly what he wanted out of life. To go somewhere where he could really make things better.

She fell silent, wondering what the Rafe of seven years ago would say if he could hear his future self talking this way. He'd probably have scoffed, never envisioning such a quiet, tame life for himself. The Ellie she had once been might have reacted the same way.

They'd changed. Both of them.

She'd worried that Rafe's wartime experiences might have altered him—maybe dug away some of his kind, optimistic streak. And perhaps they had. But in its place, had they left an even deeper well of empathy? Maybe the changes she was already sensing were for the better—making him an even more amazing, lovable man than he'd been before.

No. Stop with the love!

She wasn't going to let herself fall in love with him again so easily. After seven years away—seven years spent in hell—Rafe was still something of a stranger to her. She would never have fallen head over heels for a stranger she'd met today at the airport, and she couldn't let herself fall for Rafe again, either. Not without making sure of who he was, not without being certain the man she'd once loved still lived within that weary, jaded frame. Or at least making sure the man he'd become was someone she could trust enough to love. And who would love her back.

Finally, figuring he was probably worried at her silence, she said, "So did I mention I spent a year in Africa working on an animal preserve?"

He took his eyes off the road long enough to gape at her. "Seriously?"

"Yep. I enrolled in a special international cooperative— kind of like Doctors Without Borders, but for veterinarians. I spent a year in Kenya, helping the locals boost the elephant population."

"Isn't your specialty small animals?"

"They'll take any help they can get." She grinned. "And baby elephants are small."

"Not quite as small as a Chihuahua."

"No, I suppose not. But they're just as cute."

He continued to consider it, seeming genuinely surprised.

"What, you assumed I'd be diagnosing parakeets losing their feathers and neutering strays for the rest of my life?"

"You can do anything you set your mind to, El," he said, his tone serious—and complimentary. "I'm not at all surprised you wanted to go out and make a difference somewhere."

"Thank you. I guess I was just trying to say, I really do understand where you're coming from."

"I guess you do. What about now?"

"I work for a small-animal hospital in the city. No elephants, but one of my clients has a pretty feisty ferret."

"Are there any other kinds of ferrets?"

"Good point."

They'd fallen into an easy conversation, and she remembered that it had always been easy to talk to Rafe. They'd spent hours talking about a lot of nothing in the old days, and she'd never been bored. He was one of those people who listened and never judged or needled. Rafe was easy to be around…a strange quality for a soldier, she imagined.

She had a million more questions she wanted to ask, mainly about what his personal life had been like for the past three years, but the storm suddenly decided to pick up some steam. The snow that had been falling in thick, lazy plops, returned to its stinging pellets, and the windshield wipers struggled to clear it. Within mere minutes, the road became a slushy, icy mess. Rafe required his full concentration to keep them on the highway and they both fell silent.

There were a few dicey moments when the car tried to fishtail around one poorly marked curve. But he kept things under control.

"There should be a few hotels at the next exit," she finally said, hoping they'd come far enough that there would be something available. "Maybe we should try again?"

"Good idea."

They got off at the next exit. They'd already moved well past the Poconos, but judging by the billboards for rooms with heart-shaped beds and champagne-glass hot tubs, this place was competing for the honeymoon crowd, too. She lifted a brow as they passed some signs advertising places with names as dubious as The Little Love Nest.

They struck out at the first two chain places they tried. Then, at the third establishment, a no-name, local motel, they found someone else who spied Rafe's fatigues—and his fatigue—and wanted to do something to help out a G.I. trying to get home for Christmas.

"You say you're going to try to make it all the way t'Chicago tomorrow?"

"That's right," Rafe replied. "We're trying our best to get home to our families for Christmas."

"How long's it been, young man?"

"I haven't seen my folks for Christmas in three years."

The elderly man frowned and shook his head. "Holidays…they was always the worst. I don't usually do this— rentin' out our best room without reservations—but I can see when a man's been about wrung out. I suspect you need a good night's sleep more than I need that vacant room."

"Really?" Rafe asked, sounding hopeful for the first time in hours.

"Really. I don't think anybody's out there gettin' married tonight who might want our honeymoon suite."

Ellie's eyes rounded. *Honeymoon suite?* She intentionally turned away, not wanting Rafe to see her reaction.

"I want you to get a decent night's rest before you go back out into that storm."

Rafe nodded slowly, eyeing the gray-haired, grizzled man. "So, Vietnam?"

"Korea," the stranger replied. He walked out from behind the counter, and it was then she noticed his limp.

"Left my right leg in the Chosin Reservoir, but got outta there alive."

She fell silent, sensing an immediate bond of brotherhood arise between the two men. Both of them had been forged in battle, understood things about humanity that she and most civilians never would. The men obviously recognized in each other a kindred spirit.

"Thank you for your service, sir," Rafe said, his tone utterly respectful.

"And thank you for yours, son."

The men shook hands, connected in a way that few people ever would be with a stranger. Then the man handed Rafe a room key. "You folks have a good night, you hear?"

Ellie smiled at him and waited until they were back outside, battling the wind to get to the car, before she said, "Only one room, huh?"

She heard the nervousness in her own voice and hated herself for it. She sounded like some kind of hysterical virgin, as if Rafe couldn't be trusted with her virtue for one snowed-in night. Which was pretty ridiculous, considering she'd spent the past several hours thinking about how desperately she wanted to seduce him. Just sitting beside him in the dark, inhaling his scent, all warm and masculine, made her want to bury her face in his throat and kiss her way down his neck.

Perhaps it was anticipation making her nervous. Because, oh, she did not want to do this wrong. People only had so many opportunities to right the mistakes of the past. If she and Rafe screwed this up again, they might never have another chance.

Of course, she wasn't sure if he even wanted to try. All her thoughts and car fantasies were well and good, but if he wasn't interested, she was going to be one disappointed, frustrated woman tonight.

"I'm sorry about that," he said as he yanked open her

door and helped her get into the car. He went around to his own side and got in, the clunky, old-fashioned room key dangling from his fingers. "I didn't think to ask if you wanted to keep driving to try to find a place with two available rooms."

"No, I don't," she said with a shudder.

"If it's too uncomfortable for you, I'll sleep on the floor. Wouldn't be the worst place I've slept, and I'm so tired, I won't even notice."

"Let's check out the room before we decide," she said.

She didn't add that the bed would have to be lumpy and disgusting for her to kick him out of it...and that, if it were, she'd go with him and sleep on the floor. It was a little too risky still to make it obvious she was thinking of seducing him tonight.

"I'm not sure about this place," he said, eyeing the broken floodlight on the roof and the dilapidated sign.

The tired, roadside motel wasn't going to win any diamonds from AAA, but it was the best they could hope for under the circumstances. The smart people had gotten off the road a few hours ago, when things started to get really bad. It certainly wasn't Rafe's fault that there was no room at the inn.

She chuckled.

"Something funny?"

"Tomorrow's Christmas Eve, so it's somehow appropriate that we've found no room at any of the inns...Joseph."

He caught her reference. "I hope the honeymoon suite isn't in the stable."

"Me, too."

"Just don't go giving birth tonight, Mary."

The teasing note in his voice died even as the sentence left his lips. He cast a quick, curious glance down her body, as if checking to see if it had ever thickened with pregnancy. It amazed her that they'd spent so many hours together in a small car, yet she'd managed to avoid revealing much of anything about the life she'd lived during the past few years.

She suddenly wanted to. Needed to if they were to ever have another chance, not just for a sexual reunion but for an emotional one.

He was leaving the military. The wanderlust and hunger for danger and adventure had seeped out of him, along with some of his youth and optimism. He was home. For good. And so far the changes she'd noted in him seemed to have been for the better.

So maybe there would be room for her in his new life, and maybe she could allow him back into her heart. She still wasn't ready to completely lower her guard and flat-out ask him if he wanted to try again, but she could at least set his mind at ease about a few things.

"I don't have any kids, Rafe."

He nodded slowly, steering the car around the building, carefully easing past a long line of cars parked haphazardly between snowdrifts. He never looked over, though. She knew he needed to concentrate, but she suspected it was more than that. In fact, she suspected he hadn't wanted her to see how much her words had pleased him.

If those had, she couldn't imagine how he'd feel about the next confession.

"Here we are," he said as he pulled up outside the squat cement building, the headlights illuminating the door of room number 128. The car shuddered a little as it slid into the parking spot.

She nodded, taking a deep, relieved breath that they really had found a place to weather the storm. Once inside, she could tell him the rest—tell him she hadn't married Denny, that their breakup had been one of the reasons she'd decided to go off to Africa, seeking some of the adventure he'd been so desperate to find.

"I can't wait to get into a warm place and stay there," she

said, flexing her feet and her legs. They were practically numb, both from the cramped quarters and the cold, which had seeped in despite the car heater's best efforts. It was very late. Between the snowy roads and the stops to look for a hotel, they'd been traveling for almost seven hours.

"Be careful, it's very slippery," he said. "Wait and let me come around and help you."

Grabbing her carry-on bag from the backseat, she reached for the door handle. "Don't be silly, you're talking to a Chicago girl," she insisted. "I eat snow for breakfast."

"Hopefully not the yellow kind," he said with a grin.

A real one. A sexy, old-Rafe, genuine one.

Oh, God, the man she'd loved really was lurking inside there, just wrapped in a more serious, introspective package.

Opening the door, she stepped out into the night, the icy snowflakes hitting her face in a painful little barrage. She threw a hand up to ward them off, and suddenly lost her balance. Her feet skidded, her warm boots doing absolutely nothing to keep her steady, and she began to fall. Grasping for the car, she tried to stop her descent, but her gloved fingers grabbed only air.

Rafe must have leaped over the hood because he was there, catching her in his arms, before she hit the ground.

"Holy crap," she whispered, shocked at how quickly it had all happened—within a matter of seconds.

"I've got you," he said, holding her tightly against his body. He'd skidded onto his own knees when he grabbed her, landing hard, but protecting her from harm. There might be several inches of snow on the ground, but it wouldn't have provided much of a cushion if she'd slammed down on his hip.

"Maybe you should have practiced *walking* in snow rather than eating it for breakfast," he said, those sexy lips quirking with humor.

"Maybe. I can't believe you caught me. You must have flown over the hood."

"You should have waited."

"I'm sorry. Thank you."

Their eyes met, their stares holding, despite the snow and the wind and the crazy location. His body radiated heat through the thick layers of clothes. She was closer to him than she'd been in years, sharing his breath, seeing the steady pulse beating in his neck.

Unable to help herself, needing to taste him to get one last, final confirmation that he really was here, she tilted her head and brushed her lips against his, not sure of where she got the nerve but not questioning the impulse.

He resisted for no more than a second, then drew her even more tightly against his body. He opened his mouth, thrusting his tongue against hers in a deep, hungry exploration that both shocked and thrilled her. Ellie kissed him back with fervor, loving the familiar taste of him, that unique Rafe flavor that she'd never experienced with any other man she'd kissed.

The icy snow pelted them and the wind blew so hard her ears hurt, but they kissed and kissed, turning their heads to take things even deeper, urged on by the desperation of so many long, lonely years.

A horn beeped somewhere, long and low, the sound echoing across the thick night. Startled, Rafe pulled away. He stared at her, opened his mouth to say something. No words emerged. Their stares held. Finally, he merely sighed.

"Let's go inside," she said, knowing he was thinking that she was a cheating wife and blaming himself for doing something so dishonorable.

"I'm sorry. I should never have…"

"Please, Rafe, take me inside," she insisted. "We've got some talking to do. You're going to want to hear what I'm going to say."

She only wondered what was going to happen once he found out she was not only unmarried...but single and completely available.

Not to mention willing.

4

R<small>AFE HAD NO IDEA</small> what Ellie planned to tell him. What could she say that would make him feel any worse than he already did?

He'd broken the guy's code. Decent men didn't go around kissing other men's wives. Even wives who had carved out a piece of your heart and held it in their grasp for seven years.

It had been the heat of the moment, that was all. Adrenaline. She'd almost fallen, he'd saved her from a nasty spill, she'd wound up in his arms.

One kiss. No big deal in the scheme of things.

Even if, in his heart, he knew that kiss had been a *huge* deal, if only because it left him with a hunger for more.

Saying nothing, he rose to his feet, staying grounded with not only his own weight, but hers. He didn't immediately put her down, not ready to let her risk another fall. Or not ready to let her out of his arms. Which one, he couldn't say.

Walking carefully, hearing the crunch of his thick-soled boots in the snow, he carried her to the door of their room and then lowered her onto her own feet. Inserting the thick key into the stiff, icy lock, he kept one arm on her shoulder to be sure her feet didn't slip out from under her. Although there was an awning that extended the length of the building, the snow had drifted and icy flakes attacked them.

"One more second," he told her as he jiggled the key, which resisted within the lock. He finally got it to disengage, grabbed the handle and twisted. Finding utter blackness within, he reached around the corner, groping for a light switch. Finding it, he flipped it up and the room gained a sickly yellowish tinge.

"Yikes. Maybe you should have left the light off," she said, eyeing the room dubiously as they walked inside and pushed the door shut behind them.

"Beggars can't be choosers. It's better than a stable, isn't it?"

She snickered, continuing to study the room, which could only be described as roadside-no-tell-motel chic. The worn, shag carpeting was a faded orange color that had probably been cool and hip in the 1960s…when it was installed. The flimsy furniture consisted of a dresser with two sagging drawers, a table and two mismatched chairs.

But the bed. Oh, the bed.

It was huge—California king, he'd say. It was made up with a red velvet spread, and above it, attached to the ceiling…

"Oh. My. God."

He whistled, mentally echoing Ellie's exclamation.

Because the ceiling of this entire room was mirrored.

"I guess this is why it's called the honeymoon suite," she said, sounding as though she were forcing the words out of a very tight throat.

He understood the reaction. His own throat suddenly clenched, because all he could imagine was the two of them on that bed, all night long. With those mirrors above them, and the door closed to the storm…and the entire world.

"I'm pretty sure this room has been used in every episode of *Supernatural*," she said, averting her gaze from the bed. As if she feared Rafe would think she was worrying about sleeping in it with him. Or that she *wasn't.* "Sam and Dean always stay in one like it."

"Even with only one bed and the mirrors?"

"Well, maybe not *just* like it."

He rolled his eyes, chuckling. "Still into that spooky stuff, huh?" he asked as he tossed his duffel onto the dresser. He had also grabbed her carry-on, which had landed in the snow, and now put it beside his things.

"The spookier the better. Still only like to read nonfiction?"

"I've expanded my tastes a little," he admitted. "Believe it or not, one of the guys in my unit has a sister who sends him cases of romance novels every so often. They really make the rounds and are usually worn out from rereading."

She burst into laughter. "A bunch of tough army rangers reading romance novels."

Yeah, it sounded pretty strange. Then again, considering the lives he and his squadmates lived, maybe something easy and familiar—something that lifted the spirits and reminded them of the girl back home—was perfectly normal after all.

"Do they read the super sexy ones?" she asked, her tone a little too innocent. Huh. He wondered if she asked because they'd just kissed as if they were about to make use of every inch of mirror above them.

"Those were the most popular ones," he admitted with a wry grin. "Some of them are damned good. Plus it gets pretty lonely in the field when fraternization is strictly prohibited."

"So, how long has it been since you've…fraternized?" she asked, again, obviously striving for friendly curiosity rather than any kind of personal interest.

He wasn't buying it. She was interested. She shouldn't be, he shouldn't want her to be. But he felt it. Awareness sizzled and crackled in the cold room like sparks jangling off exposed wire.

"A long time," he admitted.

She stepped closer, eliminating the space between them, and every step she took messed with his head a little bit more, until he could barely remember what the words *nice* and *guy* meant.

She licked her lips before asking, "Does that mean you're not involved with anyone?"

He shook his head, his amusement fading, his jaw growing a little stiff. "No. Unlike you, Mrs…"

"Actually, it's Doctor, remember?"

"Sorry. Doctor what?"

"Doctor Blake."

"Didn't take his name, huh?"

Ignoring the question, she tugged her gloves off her hands. She'd been wearing them all evening, since the heater in the rental car hadn't quite managed to chase out the cold. Still silent, she brushed her soft fingertips across the small scar on his jaw. It had been joined by another on his temple—one he knew looked newer, rawer—and she gently caressed that one, too.

Rafe literally growled in his throat. "Ellie, don't."

"I hate that you've been hurt."

He reached up and grabbed her hand, intending to push it away. But he couldn't do it. Something within him rebelled at ever pushing this woman away again. He instead squeezed her fingers, turning his face toward her palm and pressing his mouth to her skin. He kissed her, breathed her in, let his head fill with that sweet, light scent she always wore, before growling, "Damn it. You're a married woman."

"Says who? Maybe you should take another look at my left hand."

He froze. Slowly lowering their joined hands, he stared at that left ring finger. It was totally bare. Not only was she not wearing any kind of ring, there was no tan line, no crease indicating she usually wore any jewelry there at all.

His heart spun in his chest and tension coiled low in his belly. But he didn't allow the emotions to rush through him just yet. She was a veterinarian, maybe she just didn't wear a ring.

"What, exactly, are you trying to say?"

"I'm not married, Rafe."

He slowly exhaled the breath he'd been holding. *She's not married?* Ellie was free? He couldn't quite get his mind to wrap around that. He'd drilled the *she's-off-limits* message into his mind dozens of times over the past three years, during the many moments he'd longed to reach out to her. But it wasn't true?

"Are you divorced?"

"No. I never got married at all."

"Why not?"

"It just didn't work out."

His jaw flexed. "Did he hurt you?"

She laughed lightly. "Oh, God, no. Denny and I are still the best of friends—in fact, I work for him at his new animal hospital. He's married to my friend Jessie now."

Barely able to take it in, he swiped a hand through his short hair, sure it was a spiky mess. He watched her rub her fingers against her own palms, as if she were dying to reach up and stroke that hair, to twine her fingers in it and pull him down so they could get back to that kiss they'd started three years ago on New Year's Eve, continued outside and ached to finish now.

She didn't, though. Rafe was still stunned, and probably looked it, too. He'd been telling himself for hours that he'd blown his chance with her and needed to accept the fact that she would only ever belong in his past.

But he'd been wrong. Everything had been wrong. He still didn't quite believe it.

"I don't understand."

"I haven't even dated a man since Denny and I broke up almost three years ago."

"Three years…" The timing couldn't be coincidental.

"It wasn't New Year's Day," she insisted. She went on to admit, "But it wasn't too long after that, either."

"Ellie, what are you really saying?"

"I'm saying, silly man, that after I ran into you on New Year's Eve, I realized I didn't love Denny the way a woman should love her fiancé. And I also realized he and Jessie shot a lot more sparks off each other than he and I did."

Sparks were critical in a relationship, the two of them had shared enough to do more damage to Chicago than Mrs. O'Leary's cow, the rumored start of the Great Chicago Fire. How she'd thought she could happily marry someone without sparks, he had no idea. Friendship and companionship and common interests were well and good, but a relationship also needed a healthy dose of pure passion. Like the passion he and Ellie had shared once.

And still did, he strongly suspected.

"Running into you that night was the best thing that could have happened to me. It helped me see things more clearly."

"Running into you wasn't a coincidence," he admitted.

"What?"

"I knew you were going to be at that New Year's Eve party. My cousin's wife told me."

She fell silent, evaluating how she felt about his confession. Had he told her then, she might have resented him, especially because he'd sensed she was angry at him for piercing her bubble of boring contentment.

"I'm sorry," he added.

She slowly nodded, accepting the apology. "It's okay. It worked out for the best. In the end, I returned Denny's ring, and by February 14, he had a new Valentine and I couldn't have been happier."

He ran a hand over his stubbled jaw, still watching her

closely, praying he hadn't caused her any more heartache. Because, after all, wasn't his need to protect her from hurt the very reason he'd broken up with her in the first place? And hadn't he cursed his own noble instinct every day since he'd done it?

"I'm all grown up, Rafe. I've got a great job, a ton of friends. I've traveled the world. I'm happy. I'm successful. But there's one thing I don't have—one thing I haven't had in a very long time."

"What's that?"

She stepped close again, until one of her legs slid between his parted ones and their hips brushed. Lifting her hands to encircle his neck, she stared into his eyes and rocked the world beneath his feet with two simple words.

"A lover."

ELLIE WATCHED HIM absorb her words and interpret her meaning. She'd issued an invitation—or maybe a challenge. She held her breath, wondering how he'd answer it.

"Ellie, I didn't offer you a ride so we…"

"Shut up, Rafe," she said, tightening her arms around his neck. "Don't analyze it, don't explain it, don't talk about it. I don't expect anything, I'm not asking for anything beyond tonight. Tomorrow will come no matter what happens. So just make love to me like I've wanted you to for the past seven years."

He searched her face, as if memorizing her, making sure this wasn't another dream.

"I'm real. I'm here," she whispered.

"Thank heaven."

No more words were needed. With hunger that bordered on desperation, he wrapped his arms around her and hauled her up against his chest, covering her mouth with his. His lips parted, his tongue thrusting deeply against hers. She welcomed him hungrily, loving his taste, wondering how on earth she'd survived so long without it. The kiss went on and on, seven years of longing wrapped up in it, and in that kiss she found the answers to so many questions.

Yes, he still cared. Yes, they still had incredible chemistry.

Yes. Oh, God, yes, this was definitely going to happen.

Her arms tight around his neck, she let him pick her up, those strong hands gripping her hips, his fingers squeezing and then cupping her backside. She lifted her legs and wrapped them around his hips, groaning deeply as her groin struck directly against his. He was powerfully erect, and she suddenly recalled how generously he was built. She shivered, remembering how that massive shaft had filled her to the brink.

Heat flooded through her, landing between her thighs so hard she had to rub against that huge erection just to gain some relief. He thrust back, and she cooed in delight as that hot ridge hit her clit and sent bolts of pleasure rocketing through her.

"Oh, Ellie," he groaned against her mouth. "It's been so long."

"Forever."

It hadn't merely been ages since she'd had sex. But what she'd had with Denny, or with anyone else before him, just didn't compare with this intense connection she had with Rafe. There was no thinking involved here, it was all instinct and innate understanding and such pure, utter connection. He had understood how to please her the first time he'd touched her. He still knew just how to kiss her, just how to stroke her, just how deeply to plunge and how gently to lick and how firmly to caress. Everything about him seemed tailored specifically to her.

And with him, she never experienced a moment of misgiving, not the slightest hesitation. She wanted to do and to be and to explore and to indulge. She wanted his mouth on her thighs, his tongue on her clit. She wanted to lick all that male heat until he was groaning and helpless, to suck him until he couldn't remember one single day that they'd been apart.

A single snowy night somewhere in Pennsylvania could never be long enough to make up for all the nights they'd lost. But in case it was all they had—in case the passion was still there, but the emotions were not, or in case they had both changed too much to really work as a couple again—she was going to take whatever she could get tonight and deal with the fallout tomorrow.

They kissed until neither of them could breathe, tongues wild and hungry, their bodies twisting and thrusting, then drew apart to gasp for air. She continued to hold him tightly with her arms and her legs as he carried her to the bed and tossed her down onto it.

Ellie quickly jerked the covers down, pushing them out of the way, but didn't recline and beckon for him. Instead, she sat up on the edge of the bed. Rafe was bending over to take off his boots, and she did the same, her fingers shaking on the laces, every ounce of her attention on him rather than on what she was doing.

Rafe straightened and was unfastening his belt when he saw her reach for her own waistband and flick the button of her jeans. He froze, staring, and Ellie smiled a little, savoring this heady anticipation. They were both anxious—frantic, really. But, despite the fact that they'd been lovers and had shared incredible intimacies in the past, there was certainly a newness now, as if they were experiencing each other for the first time.

She was no longer a skinny college girl, she had a woman's curves and a woman's confidence. So she made sure she gave him something to look at, wanting him out of his mind with need before he so much as touched her again.

Lying back on the bed, she unzipped her jeans and wriggled out of them slowly. She thrust her hips up as if to scoot the fabric out from under her bottom, but she was in truth both issuing an invitation and making a promise.

Rafe continued to stare, his eyes glued to the tiny pink panties that remained in place once she'd pushed the denim out of the way. When she sat up enough to kick the jeans all the way off, letting her legs splay apart, he rubbed his hand on his jaw and opened his mouth to breathe deeply, trying to maintain control.

Silly man. She wanted him to forget the meaning of the word *control*.

Slowly rising again, she slipped her fingers under the elastic edge of her panties, stroking her hipbone. Rafe watched her closely, then moved his hand to his fly, flicking one button, and then another. He had to tug the material away from his stone-hard cock and she saw the way he stroked himself through his clothes as he studied her.

Rising onto her knees, she beckoned him closer.

"Let me help."

He did as she asked, saying nothing as she began to unfasten the buttons on his heavy outer shirt. When she'd unfastened it completely and pushed it off him, she stared at the light green T-shirt he wore underneath, marveling at the way the cotton molded to that incredible body.

His chest was so broad, his shoulders massive, the muscles in his arms rippling and intimidating. He seemed fully capable of breaking her in half, though she didn't have even the tiniest hint of fear. He would never hurt her. Despite what he'd been doing for the past seven years, she'd always known Rafe was a caretaker, a tender, loving protector who would sooner chop off his own hand than lift it in anger against any woman. He could never have changed enough to ever make her fear him.

She slid her hands under the bottom of his shirt, rubbing her palms against that hot, muscular stomach, and began pushing the fabric up. Delight washed through her as she stroked the ripples and ridges of his body, and she marveled at the beauty of every inch revealed.

Her breath suddenly caught in her throat, though, when she found the scars.

One was about three inches wide, on his side, between two ribs. The other was on his chest, below one flat nipple. She pulled away enough to look at them; the raw redness of the one on his ribs said the wound hadn't been there long.

"What happened?" she whispered.

"Nothing."

Tears came to her eyes as her mind tried to imagine how these marks had come to be on his body. But even these had a kind of beauty, told a story about the man he had become, so she didn't press him for details. Rafe brushed the moisture away with his fingertips, just as silent. Finally, she moved on, continuing with the shirt, pushing it all the way up. He took over, yanking it over his head and tossing it to the floor, now wearing just his partly unbuttoned pants.

She sat back on her heels, staring at him, having to remind herself to breathe. He was just so amazingly perfect, so incredibly hot, her brain forgot to work. Her heart was falling down on the job, too; her heartbeat was a staccato jangle, all thuds and leaps. She wanted to kiss and stroke every inch of him, but just wasn't sure which delicious spot to sample first.

"So," he said, "one of us is wearing too much up top and the other too much on the bottom."

She immediately pushed at her panties. "You mean these?" Yanking them down, she heard his hoarse gasp and laughed wickedly.

"Mmm, not exactly what I was referring to, but I definitely like the way you think."

"Oh, wait, did you mean my shirt?" she asked, pretending to pull the panties back up.

"Forget it," he ordered, pushing her hands away. He

hooked his own thumbs in the nylon and tugged them down.
She rose up onto her knees again so he could get them all
the way off her, loving that his hands shook as he lifted
the small bundle of fabric and shoved it into his pocket.

"Did you just steal my underwear?"

"Yeah. Do you have a problem with that?"

"Are you going to sell glimpses of them to all the other
freshmen in the boys' bathroom?"

"These are for my own personal treasure box," he promised, those dark eyes gleaming. "When I first went into the
service, I spent a whole lot of nights wishing I'd stolen a
pair right off you."

"I wish I'd had the idea to give you some," she murmured, wondering how long he'd fantasized about her before he'd finally decided to force her to let him go for good.
Somehow, she knew he'd thought about her long after he'd
made that decision. Just as she'd thought about him long
after she'd given up.

"Let's not dwell on any of that," he said. "Tonight is
like getting the Christmas gift I always wanted but never
dreamed I'd actually get. So let's just be glad for what we
have now rather than what we didn't have then."

A lump formed in her throat as she heard the emotion
in his voice. She swallowed the lump down, knowing he
was right, but she was so heartbroken for all those moments
they'd never had.

"I want you, Ellie," he said, hunger chasing away any
lingering regrets. "I'm dying for you."

She considered dragging the anticipation out some more,
building it higher, but right now, she just wanted to be
naked, wanted him naked, wanted to fill every minute they
had with erotic intimacy.

So she wasn't coy. She didn't tease. She simply reached
for the bottom of her sweater and yanked it up and off.

"God, you're so beautiful," he said, staring down at her

as if he'd never beheld anything so perfect. He couldn't take his eyes off her breasts. Her nipples were poking saucily against the lace of her bra, both from the cold and from the incredible heat he'd built within her. Remembering how much he'd loved to suck them, she traced her fingers against the puckered tips, very aware he wanted to replace her hands with his mouth.

"Show me," he demanded.

She unclasped her bra and let it fall off her shoulders. Then she was kneeling on the bed before him, stark naked, her long red hair covering her chest, though her nipples peeked between the strands. He eyed her as though she were a banquet and he couldn't decide what to taste first.

She flung her hair out of the way and lifted her breasts in her own hands, tweaking her nipples with her fingers.

"Please," she begged.

Decision made. A deliberate smile on his face, Rafe dropped to his knees on the floor and pulled her closer to him. Her parted thighs went around his waist, and he moved one hand to her breast as he caught her mouth in another kiss. Their tongues thrust and played while he tweaked and stroked her, one breast, then the other, until she was panting and gasping against his lips.

She twisted and thrust, wanting more, wanting him to suckle her, and she realized he was intentionally drawing this out when she heard his deep, evil chuckle.

"Tell me what you want," he said.

"You know very well."

"Maybe, but I'm just a simple soldier. Give me an order."

"Don't tempt me…"

He nuzzled her throat, kissing his way down to the hollow and growled, "I love tempting you."

She arched her back, pressing her breasts toward him, then gave him the command he'd been determined to wring from her. "Suck my nipples, Rafe, please. Use your mouth on me and don't you dare be gentle."

"Yes, ma'am," he replied, satisfaction oozing from him.

And oh, the man was good at following orders. He kissed his way down her chest, scraping his teeth over her collarbone. Holding both breasts in his hands, he tweaked and plucked her sensitive nipples until she was quivering. When he finally moved his mouth to one breast and licked his way down the upper slope, she whimpered. And when that mouth moved over her nipple and he suckled her, she let out a little scream of pleasure.

The sound inflamed him. As if he'd finally shaken off the last of his own restraints, he sucked her hard. She wound her fingers in his hair and held him close, crying at how good it felt. When he left her breast long enough to kiss his way to the other one, she realized she couldn't stand much more. She needed him inside her, breaking down the last of the walls between them.

She reached for his half-unbuttoned fly and began working the remaining buttons free, hearing him hiss as the back of her hand brushed against the tip of his cock. She was all sensation and electricity, every brain cell was focused only on how much she wanted him inside her—wanted that heat and that strength and that thickness.

"Wait a second," he said. "I've got condoms in my pack."

She didn't ask why, she was just thankful he had them. Considering she hadn't even given it a moment's thought, it was lucky he'd been a good soldier and come prepared.

He moved away and dug around in his bag. She watched him from a couple of feet away, admiring the play of light on his flexing muscles. From here, she was able to make out a large, military tattoo on one shoulder, and she was determined to examine it more closely later. When she had regained some semblance of sanity.

He pushed his pants off his lean hips as he returned,

sending his boxer briefs with them to the floor. Ellie let out a tiny moan, seeing how massive and proud he was, and how very much he wanted her. She couldn't resist reaching out and brushing her fingers across the throbbing tip of his cock, smoothing the moisture that had gathered there. He groaned and his eyes fell closed as he thrust into her hand, silently begging for her touch.

Ellie encircled him and stroked, up and down, squeezing him, marveling that he grew even thicker, even longer, in her hand.

"So much I want to do," he muttered, "but I have to be in you now, El."

She didn't hesitate, scooting back on the bed and lying down, her legs parted invitingly. After putting on the condom, he raked a thorough, heated stare over her body—admiration dripping from him—then moved between her open thighs. As the tip of his cock nudged against her slick folds, she arched toward him, welcoming him, crying out as he slid into her. Inch by inch he entered her, filling her with warmth and with pleasure, reminding her of all that had been missing from her life since he'd left it.

Oh, yes. This is pleasure. This is what I've longed for. Now I remember how it feels to be really alive.

She glanced up, her attention drawn to that mirrored ceiling, and suddenly understood the appeal, being able to see him plunging down into her as she thrust up to meet him. He looked absolutely gorgeous lying between her legs, the muscles in his powerful back flexing, his taut buttocks tightening, his thighs so dark against her pale ones.

"I've missed you so much," he said, staring down at her as he sank deeper and deeper. "I must have dreamed this moment a thousand nights."

Tears pricked the corners of her eyes. "Then we were having the same dreams," she admitted. "I just hope we don't wake up this time."

5

ALTHOUGH THEY HADN'T gotten nearly as much sleep as they'd intended to when they'd stopped at the motel, Rafe woke up the next morning feeling better than he had in years. Yes, he'd slept on a lumpy bed with dingy, paper-thin coverings, in an arctic-cold room, beneath some huge, cracked mirrors, but it was a palace compared to a lot of the places he'd slept in recently. And it wasn't just because he was in a bed, inside a building, rather than on a cot in a crowded barrack. No, the smile he'd been wearing on his face since the moment he woke up was caused entirely by the woman who'd slept in his arms.

Ellie was still asleep, her body wrapped around him. One slim thigh rested between his legs, her arm lay draped across his waist, her fingers brushing his hip. That glorious red hair was spread out on the pillow, a mass of tangles and curls, evidence of the way he'd buried his hands in it through the night. Her lips were swollen—so well kissed—and there were faint reddish marks on her throat and her shoulders from where he'd explored her with his mouth.

He couldn't remember another night in his life as amazing as the previous one. They'd pleasured each other for hours, drifting into short naps between intense, erotic bouts of lovemaking. He hadn't left a spot on her body untouched and she'd driven him just as crazy with that luscious little mouth.

He hated to slip out of her arms, but a soft morning light had crept in around the edges of the curtain, and a quick peek at his watch said it was after 8:00 a.m. As nice as it might be to spend the entire day in bed, he'd promised to get them both home for Christmas. He intended to keep that promise, as long as the weather cooperated.

Getting up and going into the bathroom, he returned to find Ellie tucked to the tip of her nose beneath the blankets. She eyed him accusingly. "You took the heat with you."

"Sorry," he said with a laugh.

"Warm me up."

"Yes, ma'am." He dropped the clothes he'd been about to put on and crawled in beside her. She was deliciously naked, her breasts immediately drawing his attention, the pert nipples pearly and tempting. So tempting, he couldn't resist sliding his mouth across her throat and sucking her good morning.

"Oh, my," she whispered, twining her hands in his hair. Her body arched toward him, silently demanding more. He complied, tweaking and sucking her until she was quivering, not with cold, but with pure heat.

"Rafe, please," she whispered, her voice a study in need.

"Please what?"

"Please don't stop."

"I couldn't if I wanted to," he said with a throaty chuckle. "You might rip my hair out by the roots."

She immediately unwound her fingers. "I'm sorry."

"Don't be," he insisted as he kissed his way down her belly, noticing the goose bumps but not sure whether they were from the cold or from the path his mouth was traveling.

Soon, it didn't matter. She might have been cold when he'd left her in the bed, but by the time he reached his destination and slid his tongue between the slick folds of her sex, she was on fire.

"Please," she groaned, her hips gently thrusting toward his mouth.

He'd pleasured her like this during the darkest hours of the night, but now he loved being able to see her, to thoroughly explore her secret places, to drink from her softness. She tasted warm and feminine and mysterious, and probably the only thing better than swallowing down all that sweetness was hearing her cries as she climaxed right against his tongue.

"Oh, Rafe, yes!" she cried, her nails digging into his shoulders.

Desperate to be in her before the last spasms left her, he yanked on a condom and moved over her, settling between her thighs. She welcomed him, wrapping her arms around his neck, drawing him down for a deep kiss. She must have tasted herself on his tongue, but she kissed him deeply, erotically, and that just got him off even more.

"I have to be in you," he groaned.

She widened her thighs, bending her knees and opening for him, crying out as he nudged his cock into her slick channel. She was hot and ready, tight and so damned perfect, he almost wanted to stop just to imprint the memory of her on his brain. Nobody had ever made him feel the way Ellie did, and, he was now certain nobody ever would. He was a one-woman man and she was his woman, and that was the end of it. If he couldn't have her, he didn't want anyone.

Once upon a time he'd been sure he'd lost her. After last night, though, he'd begun to question that assessment, to hope he might have his second chance after all. Maybe they could make this work.

He wanted that more than anything. More than he

wanted his discharge, more than he wanted his life back, more than he wanted a future. He just wanted Ellie.

But he didn't know if she felt the same way. Last night she'd said she wanted him to be her lover...for the night. She'd said nothing about what the next day would bring.

Staring down at her now, with him buried in her body, he cupped her cheek in his hand, rubbing his thumb across her lips. She kissed it, staring up at him, her beautiful eyes hiding nothing, and the tenderness in her expression grabbed his heart and squeezed.

He began to thrust slowly, imprinting himself on her, sure of what she wanted and what she craved. Their bodies had been made for this, created for each other, and she answered every stroke and met every tender thrust. Until, once again, they came together in a hot flood of insanity that left him never wanting to be sane again.

THEY LEFT THE HOTEL at about nine-thirty—much later than the dawn departure time they'd discussed the night before. But considering neither of them had wanted to get out of that bed, Ellie figured they'd made pretty good time.

As it turned out, it was just as well they'd slept in. During the past half hour or so, they'd heard the whirr of an engine in the parking lot. When they walked outside, they spotted the owner of the hotel riding a small lawn tractor with an attached snow blade. He was plowing out the snow behind their rental car, and offered them a broad smile when they emerged.

The snow hadn't stopped, but it had definitely slowed down, the flakes falling evenly but softly. The sky was a muted blue-gray, the sun in hiding, the clouds thick and pregnant with moisture.

"Trucks've been going by up on the interstate," the man called as he backed the tractor out from behind the car. "Weatherman's saying we're in the eye of the snow-i-cane and it's never gonna be better than it is right now. Maybe you can stay in the eye and travel with it clear on out to Chicago!"

"That was so nice of you to clear us out," Ellie said as they walked over to him.

Rafe immediately extended an arm to help the owner off the tractor. "You didn't have to do that."

"Didn't figure you'd want to spend a lot of hours digging out. Musta gotten another six or seven inches after you folks pulled in here last night."

Ellie couldn't help it. She sucked her lips into her mouth and let out a tiny bark of laughter, thinking that she'd gotten a lot more than six or seven inches last night.

Rafe glanced at her, curious. She just bit her lip harder and shook her head, aware her eyes had to be sparkling with naughtiness.

He finally caught on and a grin tugged at his lips. "Bad girl," he muttered.

"Eh, what?" asked the elderly man.

"Nothing. Not a thing. Listen, can I at least pay you for your trouble?"

"Don't you insult me, son! You and your missus get on home to your folks and have a merry Christmas, and that'll be payment enough for me."

Rafe didn't correct the man on the missus thing, and Ellie found herself warmed by that. She'd dreamed years ago of being Rafe's wife, and while those dreams had once faded, last night had brought all of them rushing back into her mind.

She had awakened yesterday morning in New York sure she knew how she would spend the next several years of her life. She'd be happy—or at least content—with her job. She'd probably meet and date men. She might even find one she wanted to marry. But she hadn't believed she'd find the once-in-a-lifetime passion she shared with Rafe, assuming she'd left that behind.

Now, the entire world seemed different. So many possibilities were spread out in front of her.

Last night, she and Rafe had proved they still had amazing chemistry. She would never, as long as she lived, have a lover as perfect for her as he was.

But now that daylight had returned—bringing with it the crazy weather, their jobs, families, expectations and the past that hovered over them like a cloud—could they really move forward? Could she risk falling in love with him all over again—with this new Rafe she was only just getting to know?

She wasn't sure. Because even after everything they'd shared throughout the long, erotic night, neither of them had broached the subject of the future. Just what was going to happen when they got to Chicago? Did Rafe see this merely as a chance to make some old dreams come true, to get some old, lingering emotions out of his system once and for all? Was she alone in wondering if the wild sex was evidence of a still-deep, abiding love? Could they possibly regain the happily-ever-after they'd once talked about, that had seemed so irrevocably lost to them?

Just because they were different people—because they'd grown, matured, even changed—didn't mean they weren't still right for each other. Or did it?

They had a day in a car to look forward to. A day to explore all the unanswered questions, to get to know each other again. And to decide where this was going.

But what if the more time they spent together, the more obvious it was that they really couldn't ever go back—couldn't revive a love that had been allowed to languish for seven years. No matter how much they might want to.

It broke her heart to even consider it. So she forced those dark thoughts away.

They thanked the innkeeper again, and then loaded their things in the car and got under way. As the man had said, the roads weren't bad. More cars were out today than there had been last night, and she imagined they weren't the only ones trying desperately to get somewhere for Christmas.

"How much farther do we have to go?" she asked once they were on the highway, making pretty decent time.

"We made it about three-hundred miles last night, so we have about another five hundred to go."

"That doesn't sound too terrible."

"If we can keep up this fifty-miles-an-hour clip, we should make it home to Chicago by midevening." He cast her a quick, comforting glance. "You should be there for that midnight eggnog toast with your family after all."

She smiled but didn't reply. Because, rather than rejoicing over that, she began to feel queasy.

Getting home to Chicago for Christmas had been the objective, so why did their likely success suddenly depress her?

Maybe it was because she still hadn't shaken this fear that whatever they had, whatever they were doing, it might not last after this trip. Yes, they were still wildly attracted to each other. Yes, the sex was absofreakinglutely amazing. But Rafe would want to go home to his family, and she would go to hers. They would thank each other, wish each other a merry Christmas…and…what?

Rafe would be home for a couple of weeks and would then leave for a year in Georgia. He hadn't wanted her to wait the last time—would he ask her to now? No, he wasn't flying off to spend years in a military zone, but Rafe was so bloody noble. He might decide that he needed to be completely free of all other obligations before he allowed himself to seriously consider a future with anyone. He might demand one more year, or insist she take it.

Or he might not want her at all. He might be too benumbed by war to let his guard down enough to let anyone back into his heart. And maybe she was too frightened to let him back into hers.

She couldn't stop thinking about it as they drove, but she did manage to put on a happy face. Twice, after asking if she was okay with it, Rafe had stopped on the highway and gotten out to help dig out a complete stranger's car. Twice her heart had melted just a little bit more as she realized that chivalrous streak was alive and well within him.

In the lighter snowfalls, when he didn't have to concentrate quite as much, they spent hours chatting lightly, mostly about family—his future niece or nephew, her relationship with Denny, Jessie and their baby. She told him about her younger sister, just a middle schooler when Rafe had left, who'd graduated from college last summer. He'd shaken his head, appearing dismayed that so much of the world had rolled on without him.

They also started talking about holidays past, and even shared their wish lists for this one. His was especially telling, including such things as a bed with no sand in it, a clock missing the 4:00 a.m. setting and a Cubs ball cap. Hers started with world peace and ended with a pair of Jimmy Choo slingbacks. She supposed his was more realistic.

Whatever changes his military experience might have wrought in him, Rafe had kept his sense of humor, and he had her laughing more than once as he talked about some of the crazy Santori family traditions he'd be walking into later tonight.

"Are you serious? There really is a feast of the seven fishes, and your family does it every year?"

"Yeah. Including smelts. Oh, God, I hate smelts. I remember as a kid I used to sneak mine onto Leo's plate."

She giggled, picturing him as a little boy.

"Tonight, one of my cousins' girlfriends—or maybe my brother's fiancée, who I haven't met—will show up with a meat-and-cheese platter. My mother will thank them and then secretly stash all the salami or pepperoni in the fridge for tomorrow."

"No meat on Christmas Eve," she said. "Got it."

As the miles flew by and they continued to talk, Ellie found herself falling further and further under Rafe's spell. She'd been stressing last night over whether he had changed beyond recognition, whether he was still the man she'd fallen in love with, only to find he was far more than that. Yes, he was sometimes hit with moments of sadness when something she mentioned struck a nerve—always something about the war, or the friends he'd lost in it. But he was also by turns funny and charming, or deep and introspective. A fully matured man, with so many facets she hadn't seen—or had been too young to recognize—in the past.

He was, in short, even more wonderful than he'd been before.

And even though just twenty-four hours ago she'd believed she would never see Rafe again, now the love she'd *always* borne for him had welled up within her like a tidal wave, engulfing her to the point where she could barely breathe.

She could no longer hide the truth from herself, or pretend there was any chance he'd changed into someone she could no longer love. There was no protecting herself from this.

She loved him. She had always loved him.

She always would.

"Here we are—Illinois at last," he said, shocking her out of her moment of utter clarity before she could do or say a thing about it.

She glanced out the front windshield, seeing they had just rolled across the border into their home state, and her heart both leaped and sank. She was happy they'd come so far in relative comfort and without any mishaps. But she also dreaded the fact that they were close to the end of their journey. She wasn't sure how to even broach the subject of their future without coming across as either desperate or pushy.

"You know what I *really* want for Christmas?" he said.

"Me, wearing nothing but a red bow?"

Okay, so that might have sounded desperate and pushy, but at least in a cute way.

"Definitely." He reached over and grabbed her hand, squeezing tightly. "But other than that?"

"Me wearing nothing but a green bow?"

His chuckle sounded pained. "Sounds as though somebody wants a little attention. Do I need to pull over and give it to you?"

She wagged her brows suggestively. "Yeah, I would love it if you pulled over and *gave* it to me."

Groaning, he shifted in his seat. "Trying to drive here."

"I don't suppose there's another hotel along this route with a room with a mirrored ceiling, huh?"

"You're killing me, El."

She dropped her hand onto his lap and he hissed. Tracing the thick ridge in his pants—oh, Lord, he was so swollen and hard for her—she sighed and quickly pulled her hand away. The driving conditions definitely weren't right for that kind of teasing.

"Sorry."

"Start checking signs for hotels with honeymoon suites," he replied, his voice thick with desire.

"Deal," she said. "Now, what is it you *really* want for Christmas?"

"A five-gallon tub of peanut butter."

It was her turn to laugh. "Should I be looking for that on the hotel sign, too? Mirrored ceiling and massive quantities of peanut butter?"

"I've missed peanut butter so much. I'll eat it off your

toes or off a spoon—or, ooh, your nipples. I could com-
bine the two things I've most missed licking over the past
seven years."

Suddenly it was her that was shifting in her seat. She
suspected he was entirely serious. The idea was intensely
arousing, but also gave her the opening she'd been searching for.

"So, you've…"

She was about to say *missed me,* but before the words
could leave her mouth, the car suddenly swerved. Rafe
muttered a curse, gripping the steering wheel with one
hand, throwing the other protectively across Ellie's chest.
She let out a yelp, seeing a car spinning wildly in front of
them. Rafe had apparently spotted it going into a spin and
tried to avoid it.

But even his excellent driving skills were no match for
the icy road and an out-of-control vehicle. They hit the
other car, spun off in the other direction and crashed into
the guardrail.

"Jesus, El, are you okay?" he immediately asked, turning and grabbing her shoulders.

"I'm fine!" she insisted. "I promise."

He ran an assessing gaze over her to make sure, then
jumped out of the car. Her heart pounded as she watched
him dash across the snowy highway, heading for the other
vehicle. They hadn't hit each other hard, but the bump had
sent the sedan all the way across into the median.

Zipping up her coat, she got out, going over to see if
she could help, too. Rafe was talking to the other driver, a
middle-aged man, who appeared completely unhurt.

"So sorry about that, man," the stranger said. "I was trying so hard to get home for Christmas, I guess I was just
going a little too fast for the conditions."

"It's fine," Rafe replied, "I'm just glad we're all okay."

Okay. And stranded on the highway at eight o'clock on Christmas Eve.

Something in her should have cried about that, felt sad, worried or concerned that they were going to freeze to death. Instead, though, Ellie could only duck her head to hide a smile. Because it didn't look as if she and Rafe were going to make it home so soon after all.

She was going to get to spend a little more time with him…hopefully enough to figure out just what was happening between them, and if he loved her as much as she still loved him.

6

As it turned out, they had the accident in a pretty good spot and were in fact less than a half mile from the nearest highway exit.

Rafe had to laugh when a police cruiser stopped to help them out and told them which town he would take them to. He'd heard of the place—his cousin Mark's wife had grown up there—and had driven past it before. But he'd never stopped.

How appropriate that he and Ellie were going to have to spend a snowy Christmas Eve stranded in a place called Christmas.

As the police officer drove them into town, they took in the animated sleighs, the costumed carolers, the wreaths, lights, twinkling trees and life-size nativities complete with donkeys, and Ellie began to smile like a kid on… well, Christmas.

"You crashed us here on purpose, didn't you?"

"I swear, I didn't," he replied.

"No better place to get stuck on Christmas Eve!" the officer said, pulling up in front of a restaurant called the Candy Cane Diner. Beyond it was the Candy Cane Inn. On the other side of the street was Candy Cane Lane. "Now you folks grab yourselves some hot coffee. If you can't get anybody out here to pick you up, head right on over to the inn. Susie, the proprietor, has plenty of room—I already radioed her."

"Thanks, officer," they said as they got out.

The diner was almost empty. Even the most diehard regulars probably preferred to spend the holiday at home with their families. As soon as they got inside and out of the wind and snow, Rafe grabbed his cell phone and called his parents.

They weren't thrilled to hear about the accident, but were happy he was so close to home. Christmas was about a ninety-minute drive from Chicago, and his brother Mike offered to come get them himself in his police cruiser.

Rafe considered it. Then he gazed at Ellie, who was eyeing a menu, trying to decide between coffee and hot chocolate, and he replied, "I hate to have you come out in this weather. We'll just ride out the storm here and you can come get us in the morning, okay?"

"Uh…us?"

He chuckled. "Didn't I mention I've got somebody with me?"

"No," his brother said, sounding very curious. "Who exactly did you bring all the way from New York in a blizzard?"

"Ellie," he admitted. "Ellie Blake."

His brother chortled and launched into a barrage of questions. Rafe ignored them, said he'd talk to him in the morning and disconnected the call. Returning to the booth, he took a seat opposite Ellie.

"I ordered one coffee and one hot chocolate. We can share."

"Good plan," he said.

"So what did your family say? Is your brother going to come pick us up?"

He shook his head. "No, not until the morning."

She didn't seem especially disappointed. "Oh, okay."

"Are you sure that's all right? You wanted to get home for Christmas."

"Tomorrow's Christmas. My family can have me tomorrow." Ellie licked her lips and dropped her eyes, as if she wasn't sure what to say.

Somehow, he already knew. He'd known all day, as they'd talked about nothing and everything, as they'd become familiar with each other again, become not just lovers but partners. They were together again. This time, nothing was going to tear them apart...not even his own hardheadedness.

The love he'd carried around for this woman for seven long, empty years, was every bit as strong today as it had been the day he'd said goodbye.

Now he wanted to tell her that.

"Tonight's for us," he said.

"Yes. For us."

He reached across the table and took her hand.

"I could try to come up with some pretty words, but I'm not the type to make speeches, and I can't think of any better way to say it than this. I love you, Ellie."

She twined her fingers with his and smiled at him so beautifully, so joyfully, his breath left his mouth in a rush.

"Really?"

"Really."

"I love you, too."

He didn't reply for a moment, letting her words sink in, letting them fill in all those empty particles where mere memory had once lived, which he'd intentionally carved out if only to survive the loss of her. Now he had her back—in his bed, in his life, in his heart—back where she belonged. Anything was possible.

"Will you wait for me? Give me one more year and then we can be together?" he asked.

She shook her head. "No."

His jaw fell open.

"No more waiting," she insisted, getting up from her seat and walking around to sit beside him on his side of the booth. "I'm coming with you."

He slid his hands into her hair and tugged her close, pressing a warm, hungry kiss on her beautiful mouth. The waitress came by, paused, then smiled and kept walking, but they didn't stop kissing. He didn't want to ever stop kissing this woman who'd owned his heart for seven years.

Finally, they broke apart, sharing breaths, heartbeats and a quiet confidence that they'd just started a wonderful new chapter of their lives.

"So you'll come with me to Georgia? As much as I hate to take you away from your job and your family, I can't be without you for another whole year."

"I'll come with you anywhere you want to go, Rafe Santori. I don't own the clinic, Denny does. He can survive without me. I'll find a place to work in Georgia—I'm sure there's some needy clinic that could use a hand."

Overjoyed, he kissed her again, sealing the bargain, happy beyond measure that he wouldn't have to be away from her ever again.

When they finally ended the kiss, he gestured out the window toward the cheerfully decorated building across the street, its vacancy sign flashing red. "There's somewhere you can go with me right now. How does Christmas Eve at the Candy Cane Inn sound?"

"Do you suppose they have mirrored ceilings?"

Laughing, he said, "I don't know. But let's ask the waitress for a jar of peanut butter to go…just to be on the safe side."

ELLIE MIGHT HAVE MISSED a midnight eggnog toast with her family, but she was sure that, for as long as she lived, last night would rank as the most wonderful Christmas Eve she had ever experienced. There had been no mirrored ceilings, no peanut butter and no seedy roadside motel with thin sheets and threadbare blankets. There had just been a warm, cozy room, a brightly burning fire in the fireplace and Rafe's strong, tender arms holding her all night long.

They'd made love for hours, whispering and dreaming and saying Merry Christmas again and again. Each time they knew they were really saying "Merry First Christmas of the Rest of Our Lives," and "Merry Last Christmas of Being Alone," and "Merry All the Christmases We Were Apart."

No presents, no carols. But oh, so much love. Enough to wipe away the memory of all the years they hadn't had together. She fell asleep whispering his name and woke to hear him whispering hers. Never in her life had she been happier.

True to his word, Rafe's youngest brother, Mike, came to pick them up the next morning. A Chicago police officer, he was driving in a well-equipped SUV and had no problem getting them to the city.

He had welcomed Ellie with open arms, as if she and Rafe had never been apart, and kept insisting that it was absolutely no trouble for her to come to Christmas breakfast with the Santoris. She'd already called her own parents, filled them in on what was happening and promised to be home by early afternoon. Rafe hadn't been with his family on Christmas for three years—she didn't want to deprive him of that for one minute longer than necessary.

When they pulled up outside, the clan was gathered on the front lawn, holding yellow ribbons and welcome banners, and she was glad she'd come along. Rafe had been happy all morning, and, of course, last night. But now, in the loving embrace of his family, he seemed completely content, as well.

They swarmed around him the moment he got out of the car. Not just his parents and brothers, but lots of Santori cousins, too, all of them shouting welcomes. Then they turned immediately to her to do the same.

She only had one sister and a few distant cousins, so she should have felt overwhelmed. But she'd gotten used to the Santoris when she and Rafe were together and found herself thrilled to be back in their midst.

"So what happened? Why did you drive from New York? And what is this about an accident?" Rafe's mother said.

"We're fine," Rafe said. "Just skidded on the ice."

"And ended up staying in the town of Christmas," Mrs. Santori said with a wink. "I hear there's magic in that place."

"I don't know about magic," he replied, meeting Ellie's eye. "But I would definitely say it's lucky."

Yes. So would she.

It was freezing out, and still snowing, so they were soon swept into the warm, happy house with all the relatives for a feast. Breakfast went on for hours, seguing from eggs and ham to pasta and roast. Ellie laughed and ate, finding herself kissed by brothers, cousins, aunts and uncles, not to mention lots of babies. All of them clambered all over Rafe, asking a million questions that he answered with patience and good humor. But he was tired, and she was glad when he slipped away by himself, probably just for a couple of minutes of peace and quiet.

"Ellie, would you please ask Rafe to come down into the rec room for a family picture?" Mrs. Santori said when they were clearing up the last of the dishes from the dining room. "I think he is in the living room, putting water in the tree."

"Of course," she said, heading through the huge house. To her surprise, she didn't trip over family members and wasn't stopped for conversation. Everybody seemed to have sifted down into the huge rec room, and she walked into the living room to find Rafe there all alone.

He was standing in front of the Christmas tree, watching the door, and as soon as she came through it, a broad smile lit up his handsome face. "There you are."

"Here I am."

He extended his hand to her. She walked over and took it, but before she could mention his mother or the picture, Rafe dropped to one knee.

"What are you…"

"I've had this for seven years." He reached into his pocket and pulled out a small velvet box.

Ellie's heart skidded and raced and she found it hard to breathe. Tears formed in her eyes.

"I bought it before I was deployed, but it didn't feel right to ask you to take it and then wait for me."

"You really…you wanted to…"

"Of course I wanted to," he said. "I'm sorry I didn't, more sorry than I can say. I regret pushing you away. I wish to God we'd had seven years of visits home and video calls and family gatherings."

"So do I. But none of that matters now. You're home and we're together. I'm not going anywhere again, not even if you say you want me to."

"I'll never do that, Ellie. I can't live without you." He flipped open the box with his thumb, revealing the perfect solitaire ring inside. "My mother has been holding on to this for me. She swore someday it would end up on the right woman's finger."

She sniffled, stunned that he'd kept this secret for so long…that, while he'd asked her not to wait for him, he had, the entire time, been waiting for *her*.

"I can't wait another minute more. Will you marry me?"

She gazed down at him, tears of pure joy in her eyes, unable to say a word. Her throat was too tight, her pulse racing too fast, her heart pounding too hard. In answer, she could only nod and extend her left hand.

He slipped the ring onto her finger. It was a perfect fit.

Then he was on his feet, taking her into his arms, kissing her passionately. She wrapped her arms around him, holding him tightly, kissing him back. Memorizing his taste, she was overwhelmed with gratitude that she would get to kiss that wonderful mouth every day for the rest of her life.

After the deep, hungry kiss ended, she was finally able to speak. "Yes, Rafe. Oh, yes, yes, yes, I'll marry you."

He laughed softly, realizing he'd shocked her into silence before and she simply hadn't been able to say a word.

"I love you so much," he said, cupping her face gently.

"And I love you. Merry Christmas, Rafe. Welcome home."

"Merry Christmas, sweetheart. Thanks for *being* my home."

His home, yes, she was. Just as he was hers.

No matter where they went, as long as they were together, they would be home.

* * * * *

JOANNE ROCK

PRESENTS UNDER THE TREE

Thank you to members of the Armed Forces
for your dedication, service and sacrifice.
I'm so grateful to you.

1

"I'M NOT SURE gold sequins and red spandex really convey the true spirit of Christmas, Ari."

Stage-show producer Arianna Demakis glanced up from her clipboard to see Krista, her best friend and also the star of her latest Vegas production, holding a tiny costume against her generous curves.

"They do in this town," Arianna teased, tugging the sequined bra top out of her friend's hand. They were lingering backstage after the last performance of *Holiday Hoopla* at the Platinum Mine Hotel and Casino. "People stay home if they want to see carolers bundled in woolen mufflers. They fly to Vegas for some sizzle."

Which Ari knew from personal experience. Captain Dylan Rivera had been looking for some sizzle four months ago when he'd blown into town for his thirtieth birthday. Seizing an opportunity to connect with a guy she'd crushed on way back when, Arianna had offered to celebrate with him in a rare impulsive moment. They'd burned up the sheets and found a passion that had left her breathless before he'd jetted off to his super-secret military deployment at some undisclosed location.

She hadn't seen him since.

"Well, suffice it to say, I'm glad you didn't put me in

the hoochie-mama number." Krista tossed the bra's matching red lamé boy shorts in a costume box that would be bound for the dry cleaners after the Christmas Eve performance of their sold-out show. "I couldn't bring myself to ask 'Whose Child is This?' while dressed like a downtown working girl."

"Not fair. The girls in those outfits sing a very adorable rendition of 'Santa Baby.' Totally appropriate." Arianna thumped her friend's shoulder with the clipboard, trying not to glance at her watch. Dylan had texted her twice in the past week, promising to make it back into town by December 25th after his in-processing…or whatever it was he had to do upon his return from overseas. He'd refused to give her any specifics, so she hadn't even been able to welcome him home when he touched down. She'd left him a ticket for the performance at the box office, but he hadn't picked it up. At 11:15 p.m. on Christmas Eve, he seemed more and more like a no-show.

"Well, I might not mind parading around like a show girl the rest of the year, but on Christmas Eve, I'm glad I got 'Winter Wonderland.'" Krista swiped a few lingering fake snowflakes from her full blond curls and pushed tortoiseshell eyeglass frames higher up on her nose. She looked more like a high-school student than a Grammy-winning singer who'd traded touring for the steady money of Vegas shows and the ability to spend more time with her steady guy, an air force lieutenant colonel who, like Dylan, was also currently deployed, but unlike Dylan, he talked with his girl Krista on Skype almost every night.

The difference in Krista's relationship with Lars and hers with Dylan stung. Arianna wished she had her life as on track as Krista did. Professionally, Arianna kicked butt and kept her world in order. On the personal side…

Not so much. Which is why she was lingering backstage on Christmas Eve.

"You can count on me to put you wherever you want, hot stuff." Arianna hugged Krista, knowing she should let her leave. The backstage area had emptied out faster than ever as the cast rushed to get home for the holiday. "Are you sure you don't mind stopping by the *Midnight Christmas Circus?*"

Arianna had three shows running in town tonight. *Holiday Hoopla* had just finished, *Magic with Noelle* would wrap in another half hour and the special single showing of the *Midnight Christmas Circus* would begin shortly in the decadent new Pompeii Theatre. She hated that she wouldn't be there in person since it was a once-a-year event and it had sold out two years in a row, but she'd planned to be with Dylan for the holiday.

Not that she expected some warm reunion after the awkward way they'd parted four months ago. They'd hardly spoken since that one night together. She understood communication could be difficult during a deployment, depending on where he'd been sent, but still…a Skype call or two would have gone a long way toward easing the awkwardness between them.

She watched a janitor sweep up a pile of loose magenta feathers, his impatient sigh a clear message he was ready to lock up and go home to his family for the night.

"Of course," Krista said. "Lars won't call me until the morning, so there's no rush for me to get home." Krista squeezed Arianna's forearms. "I'll zip backstage and make sure things are running smoothly for Maisey, or pitch in if she needs a hand. You deserve the break, Ari. Enjoy it."

Guilt nipped at Arianna for the lie she'd told her friend about wanting to take Christmas off this year. She hadn't shared the Dylan debacle with anyone, so no one also knew about her plan to break things off with him tonight.

She smoothed her hands over her straight skirt and took a deep breath, hating that she had to dissolve a relationship with a military guy after he'd been off serving his country. First she'd welcome him home, obviously. But after that… she'd tell him the truth.

"Thanks, Krista. I really appreciate it." She kept her tone light even though her frustration mounted as the minutes ticked down toward midnight. Should she admit the obvious conclusion—that Dylan wasn't showing—and just go do her job at the Pompeii tonight instead?

Krista sent her a long look. "If you'd rather have company, we could toast the holidays together."

Shaking her head, Arianna smiled and gave her friend a gentle shove toward the door. "I'm fine, and you're the best for helping me feel better about taking a break. Maisey knows what she's doing." Maisey, her assistant, had lists upon lists of details to take care of tonight. "Now go enjoy the holiday. Merry Christmas!"

"Merry Christmas." Krista hurried toward the door, blond curls bobbing on her shoulders. "I'd better get going if I want to make it before the opening curtain!"

Right. Because it was definitely late. *Midnight Christmas Circus* would be starting soon. And it was stupid and sentimental to linger backstage here any longer when the unavoidable truth stared Arianna in the face.

She'd been stood up for the holiday. How ironic.

Gathering her things, she apologized to the custodian for taking so long and strode out to the mostly empty parking lot. She didn't have far to walk; Vegas didn't do as much business this time of year. Instead, the locals ventured out to the shows during December, snapping up deals on tickets and enjoying a town normally overrun by tourists. Other years, Arianna would be grateful for the once-in-a-blue-moon lull in her business. But not this year when it meant going back to her decorated condo by herself, her foolish hopes proven to be the pipe dreams they were.

That tree she'd put up alone was going to mock her

all night. In hindsight, it had been foolish to go Christmas crazy for a guy she needed to break up with. But she couldn't get over the fact that he'd been overseas serving and that he deserved a warm homecoming, if only to honor their old friendship. They had been really good friends once.

"Ari!" a male voice called from far off.

Turning, she expected to see the custodian chasing her down. Had she forgotten something?

"Arianna!" the shout came again, but no lights shone from the closed backstage door.

The sound hadn't come from there, anyway. Confused, she clutched her purse tighter and hastened her pace. She didn't expect a street thug to know her identity, but who would be following her in a dark parking area—

"Dylan?" She hated the surge of hope in her chest. If she ended up mugged because of a wishful heart, she was going to be so angry at herself.

And him.

The sound of footsteps pounding the pavement became clear. Became closer. Whoever it was was running toward her.

She sidled closer to her car and got out her keys to unlock the door so she had a safe exit....

"Arianna?" the voice shouted again.

So familiar now. So close.

"Oh, my God." Relief flooded her, along with a mix of other emotions all tangled together. She could distinguish his outline in the gloom now as he ran through the darkness. Recognized the proud way he carried himself. "Over here!"

She clicked the panic button on her car for a split second, just long enough to light up the vehicle and sound the horn.

The speeding footsteps picked up pace.

"You can slow down," she warned him. "I'm right here."

The last word barely made it out of her mouth when

Dylan all but barreled into her, throwing the brakes on his feet at the last second so he skidded to a stop a couple of inches from her. His face was suddenly visible in the glow of street lamps—the straight slash of eyebrows, the closed, serious expression.

"I had a friend drop me off out front, but the valet told me you had a VIP spot back here." His warm male presence was suddenly far too close. "It's not midnight yet. I kept my promise."

Her heart thudded a heavy beat, her whole body aware of him and the spicy scent of his aftershave.

How could she stay mad at an air force officer returning from a deployment in a war zone? She wouldn't ruin his homecoming.

"Welcome home, Captain." She dropped her purse on the trunk of her car and wrapped her arms around his neck.

He studied her in the dim light, angling his head back to—she thought—try to see her better. Seriously? That was it? She'd expected a kiss. But wasn't that why she was going to break up with him? Because she kept expecting things she was never going to get?

Needing to know, she lifted up on her toes and brushed her mouth over his. Warmth tingled along her lips and all through her veins. Memories of their limbs entwined, their bodies seeking each other over and over again through that one night they'd spent together, made her body go loose in spite of the tension between them.

The kiss went to her head faster than a straight shot of the tequila Krista favored for birthday toasts. It had been *so long* since Arianna had been with Dylan. So much longer since she'd been with anyone else. In one night, Dylan Rivera had uncovered all her erogenous zones and made her wonder how she could ever be with any other man again.

A soft whimper of want sounded in her ears, and she realized *she'd* made that hungry noise. Did she have no self-control at all? Pulling away, she became aware of her surroundings again. She was pinned between the trunk of her Buick and the hips of a sexy officer in a dark flight suit.

More than that, he seemed to be untwining her hands from his neck. The rejection stung, until it occurred to her that he was feeling his way along her fingers.

Specifically, her ring finger.

When he came to the simple filigree band that rested there, he released a pent-up breath.

"You're still wearing the ring." His observation was matter-of-fact. Remote, even.

But then, he'd never been the kind of guy to show his emotions. His gray eyes missed nothing, however.

"We are still married," she reminded him, knowing the delicate silver symbol wouldn't be staying there for much longer now that he was home. "Or did you forget?"

"Waking up married to a woman I hadn't seen in over a decade?" His lips moved in a way that might be as close as the man ever came to a smile. "I definitely didn't forget."

2

His wife.

Dylan stole another look at Arianna's profile as she drove them through the Vegas backstreets toward her condo. Christmas lights mingled with the usual neon glitter. One lamppost featured a cowboy Santa with a lasso. Another street lamp had a banner of a tree decorated with poker chip ornaments. Familiar with navigating the city, Arianna circled behind the Bellagio and left the Strip behind.

He was grateful she'd driven. After not seeing her for months, it gave him a chance to devour her with his eyes. Greek ancestry gave her dramatic features, from her dark eyes to the thick waves of raven hair she streaked with vivid crimson. Not many women could carry that off and make it look elegant, but on Arianna, it worked. Everything else about her was so refined, from her feminine skirt to the gold hoops in her ears, that the streaked hair seemed a nod to the girl she'd once been. He remembered when her personal heroines had been kick-ass video-game sirens and not award-winning singers who could headline the shows she produced.

He still couldn't believe this sexy Vegas power broker—a producer with three different shows currently playing in town—had married *him,* a certified geek who'd gone into the U.S. Air Force for the cool tech.

A geek who'd accomplished his professional goals so thoroughly that now he couldn't breathe a word about his work to anyone, not even his wife.

Arianna Demakis had been a friend in high school—a girl who'd gotten under his skin because she'd been smart and worldly while other seventeen-year-old girls were testing the limits of how many school days they could skip and still get into the colleges of their choice. He and Arianna had gone to the senior prom together as more of a business deal than a romantic date. Even though he'd thought she was mega hot, he'd also been very aware she was out of his league and, at seventeen, he'd already had his eye on a military career that would consume him 24/7 for more than a decade.

After the prom, they'd gotten milk shakes alone instead of beers with the rest of their class, and they'd traded future agendas while they drove around their tiny hometown in southern California. Arianna's life had been as clearly mapped out as his—though in a vastly different direction with her dream of a career in theater. But they'd made a teasing bet they'd look each other up when their lives slowed down—once they reached the ancient age of thirty.

He hadn't expected her to respond to his invitation to have drinks with him and his friends when that milestone had actually rolled around. But since she worked in Vegas anyway, she'd shocked the hell out of him by showing up.

"You must be exhausted," she said, breaking the silence in the car. She wove past a bus, and he noticed her long fingers were curved around the steering wheel at precisely ten o'clock and two. But then, she did most things with textbook precision. "Did you have a long flight?"

She'd slid black leather gloves on her hands, or else his eyes would have been drawn to the wedding band—an inexpensive ring he'd chosen at a jewelry store inside the Hard Rock Hotel and Casino where they'd celebrated his birthday. It wasn't a traditional ring with a diamond, just a simple band. But then, they hadn't done a traditional wedding. For that matter, the drinks they'd been downing that night sure hadn't been of the milk-shake variety.

"I got back to the States two days ago, but I had to land at another base first for processing." Kind of. The less he offered about his work the better, but that sometimes made it tough to hold up his end of a conversation. "I have a week before I return to duty."

With any luck, there wouldn't be a lot of talk happening in that week anyhow. The tension thrumming between them after that kiss assured him the spark hadn't faded in the four months they'd been apart.

"I'm just glad you made it home for Christmas." She switched her blinker on for the turn into Dean Martin Drive. "I worried when I didn't see you after the show."

Because she cared about him? Or because she'd been waiting to end their farce of a marriage in person? He'd been coordinating the logistics for ops in a war zone for the better part of the past year, which didn't scare him half as much as finding out the answer to that question. Which was why he didn't bother to ask her.

"I would have called if I wasn't going to make it," he said.

Dylan didn't make promises lightly. The promises he made, he kept. End of story. Still, he wasn't going *there* yet. "You've got a spot in the Panorama Towers?"

"A gift to myself to celebrate five years in business." She glanced up at the side-by-side towers overlooking the Strip and he recognized shades of the girl he'd known back in high school—an awkward beauty with big dreams, a girl smart enough to be in the chess club with him but socially savvy enough to organize the small club into national-level tournament contenders. "It's a little over-the-top in some ways, but it's what people expect when they do business with my production company."

"It seems safe." He liked the place right away for that reason. He liked it even more when she pulled up to valet parking and greeted the guy who ran out to park her car. Las Vegas wasn't crime-ridden by any stretch, but the high number of tourists and the "what happens in Vegas stays in Vegas" legacy ensured there were plenty of drunken troublemakers on the prowl even in the best neighborhoods.

"I suppose it is." She tugged her purse and a briefcase out of the trunk while he hitched a worn leather messenger bag over one shoulder.

"Thanks for letting me stay with you for a few days while we…figure things out." He hadn't meant to bring that up, but as he walked with her to the elevators, it seemed as if some kind of acknowledgment was in order. Hell, he was going up to her place with a toothbrush in his bag—something needed to be said.

"I'm glad you're here. We might as well enjoy Christmas together before we…you know. Fix the mistakes from our last visit." Her coal-dark eyes darted everywhere but at him. "You said you have an apartment in Henderson?" She pressed the button for the thirty-eighth floor.

Clearly he wasn't the only one not ready to talk about that ring he'd put on her finger. He wasn't surprised she'd called it a mistake after the way he'd left her four months ago.

He'd had to get back to work, and so he'd awkwardly told her to keep the ring and that they'd figure things out when he came home at the end of the year. Guess the reckoning had arrived.

"My place is more like a hotel than a home, but yeah," Dylan responded. "It's a place to crash."

He followed her into the empty elevator car, appreciating the privacy of being sealed behind closed doors with her, even if she was already contemplating how to give him back that silver band.

In deference to the cooler temperatures this time of year, she wore a dark cape that fell open over a straight, red skirt with a long slit up one thigh. Her high leather boots covered up to her knee, but when she walked, he could glimpse a hint of stocking-clad thigh. She was a striking woman. The rich colors of her hair, her strong features and her above-average height made her stand out wherever she went.

He debated how long to wait before he touched her. Kissed her. He'd held back when he first saw her in the parking lot, unsure what his reception would be in light of the fact that they'd…married. Hell, he still couldn't believe it.

"I know this is awkward," she said suddenly, breaking the silence abruptly and making him realize he'd been gawking at her as if they were still teenagers. "But in spite of everything, I'm really glad you're home for Christmas. I mean—back in the States."

Guilt swamped him. He'd actually been back on U.S. soil twice since the last time he'd seen her. He hadn't been able to tell her that, of course, plus his job made it tough to explain what he was even *doing* there.

"I hated leaving the last time." That was the truth.

The elevator slowed to a stop, the doors swishing open and saving him from having to say any more.

Casanova he was not. And since he'd married the hottest woman he'd ever met, he figured talking would only send her running to file divorce papers all the sooner. He needed time to plot a strategy with this careful, methodical woman. Tapping into her impetuous side last time had been an unexpected surprise. He knew lightning wouldn't strike twice.

"So maybe, for the sake of the holiday, let's just enjoy

the day together and not worry about our future." She adjusted the strap of her bag on her shoulder, keys in hand. "No need to ruin Christmas with—"

"Right." He didn't want to hear her say it. "I'm all about living in the moment." He followed her out into the hall toward her unit. She had the door unlocked by the time he reached her side and he stood close to her as she opened it. Her hair smelled of citrus and spices. He wanted to bury his nose in the lush waves and forget all about the past 122 days.

"Merry Christmas." Holding the door open wide so he could see into the condo, he spotted the tree that reached almost to the ten-foot ceiling. It was a brightly lit pine centered in a window overlooking the Strip.

The decorative white lights on the tree served as sole illumination for the condo, but between them and the neon shine from the casinos coming through the floor-to-ceiling windows, the condo glowed.

The effort she'd made to decorate touched him. He'd be willing to bet she wouldn't have normally dragged a real tree—a nine footer at least—into her place if it hadn't been for his visit. They'd both been longtime loners. She because she'd never been close with her family. He because his mom had died young and his dad had moved out of the country to start over as soon as Dylan had turned eighteen.

"You did this for us?" He walked in to the scent of pine, moving toward the twinkling lights like a kid hypnotized by presents.

She slid off her coat and tossed it onto a high-backed bar stool along with her purse as she made her way into the living area. The sleekly furnished, modern apartment remained in shadow, but he recognized the dull gleam of granite counters and marble floors as well as the clean lines of Asian-inspired furnishings.

"After the way we bounced around like a couple of teenagers on your birthday, I figured your life must be as low on rituals as mine." She folded her arms across her sheer lace blouse and stared at the tree as if trying to make sense of a complex puzzle.

He set aside his bag and wished he'd had time to change out of his uniform. His rumpled flight suit was still covered with dust, while she looked as if she could have stepped off the stage, even though she worked behind the scenes at her shows.

"This is only our third date," he said, "and I've celebrated more personal life rituals with you than I have with anyone else since I became an adult."

"Does that mean we're still supergeeks, just like in high school?" She tucked a handful of thick, dark wavy hair behind her ear so she could look at him out of the corner of her eye. "Because I have to say that makes us sound really socially inept."

"Guilty as charged." He reached out to adjust the feather on a crimson bird that decorated the tree. Actually, the whole thing was full of birds, now that he studied it more carefully. Chickadees and cardinals, hummingbirds and blue jays all congregated on the branches.

"I'm guilty as charged, too." She walked over to a buffet table and switched on some kind of whole-home sound system. Classical guitar drifted through the place with a "Greensleeves" rendition.

He tried to focus on her words and not on her slim, feminine silhouette. And that hair…

Wow. He could swim laps through that hair.

"Come on," Dylan teased, leaning a shoulder against one floor-to-ceiling window as he took in the long view of her condo. "You're a gorgeous single woman in a business that showcases beautiful women. You must get hit on constantly."

"You make me sound like a brothel owner." She flipped

on the light switch above the range and dug through a cabinet until she came out with a tin of tea. "And I'll have you know that I disappear when standing next to show girls dressed in nothing but feathers and a smile, so, no, I don't get hit on all that often. Want some peppermint tea?"

Nodding, he wandered around her place, trying to get a better sense of who she was—this high-school friend who could put him at ease and in the same breath make him want to peel her clothes off and take her to bed. It was a unique combination of easiness and arousal to be around her, the same feelings she'd always inspired in him.

"Still, I'm not buying that you're a social misfit anymore, Ari."

"Then how's this?" She turned the heat up under a kettle on the gas range. "I'm successful in my business because I have a reputation for being hard-nosed and driven. I don't flirt because it complicates business relationships. Some women know how to walk that line, but I don't. So I am purposely businesslike, which has given me a reputation for being aloof. Haughty, even. The only men *that* kind of reputation attracts are arrogant guys who, frankly, I wouldn't dream of dating."

He was starting to get a better picture of who she was in her work world. His gaze roamed a series of flyers for Vegas shows that were framed on an interior wall. There were a couple for dramatic productions and one for a magic show, but the majority were big, splashy performances with titillating photos and suggestive captions. But then, this city wasn't known for tame entertainment.

"That's kind of the same way you were in high school— every guy's dream, but they were too scared to approach you."

She made a dismissive gesture with her hand. "You weren't scared."

Reaching into a kitchen drawer, she withdrew two pens

and used them to anchor her heavy hair in a knot at the base of her neck. The move was so quick and efficient he imagined her doing the same thing every day when she got home from work. He liked seeing her in her space, liked knowing her habits.

"The hell I wasn't scared of you. Hanging out with you at chess tournaments or comparing notes about how far we'd made it in *Final Fantasy X* were the highlights of my weeks. I was terrified of jeopardizing that by asking you to prom, but then again…" It was an effort not to let his eyes roam all over her smoking-hot body to make his point, but he wasn't a high-school kid anymore. "It seemed like I was doing the world a favor if I could get you in a strapless dress. You lit up the gym a whole lot more than the aluminum-foil stars."

"And you can blame sweet talk like that for our getting hitched at a drive-through chapel window."

He winced even though her comment had been lighthearted.

"It was a surreal night, that's for sure."

"The funny part is, I see people do things like that all the time, since I work in the industry. But I would have never expected I'd…" She trailed off, lifting one shoulder in a halfhearted shrug. "I wish our wedding photos had come out better, though." She reached into the same drawer where she'd found the pens and tugged out a handful of black-and-white four-by-six-inch prints. The pictures were grainy and dark, but they showed Ari and Dylan laughing in the backseat of the chauffeured convertible they'd rented that night. "I would have liked to have a good memory of the one night I was impulsive."

"One night? You must be working too hard, Ari."

"Maybe." She moved toward the kettle as it started to whistle.

He wondered how much to say, how much to push his

own agenda and how soon. But hadn't he asked her to marry him because he'd just recently learned life was too damned short to live conservatively?

"I never told you the story behind that night."

"I'm pretty sure it started with tequila shots." She poured the tea and brought steaming mugs toward the sofa facing the Christmas tree. Beyond that, a window framed the view of the strip from the thirty-eighth floor.

"It started before that." He studied her profile as she leaned forward to settle the heavy stoneware mugs on a tray centered in the middle of a leather ottoman.

"What do you mean?" She settled on the sofa and clutched her cup.

He watched her take a sip. Waited.

And hoped for the best.

"There was a close call the week before my birthday."

In the silence that followed, she straightened. Leaned forward.

"As in…?" she finally prodded.

"A hairy situation in the air." Even months later, he still broke out in a cold sweat thinking about it. "It was a practice drill, but the potential for danger was very real with the kind of exercise we were running—a minimum-interval takeoff where we send up aircraft as quickly as possible."

"What happened?" She slid out of her shoes and tucked her legs to one side beneath her on the couch. The slit in her skirt parted, giving him a generous view of one slim thigh.

He drank in the sight of her, feeling anchored somehow by her presence.

"We got into the slipstream of the aircraft ahead of us and the plane jumped. Nearly flipped." His gut rolled with the memory. "I've been in battle situations that didn't mess with my head the way that moment did. It was disorienting. Totally out of my control." Worse, all the tech had gone down for a god-awful minute, freaking him the hell out.

That should have been the least of his concerns when the aircraft was almost inverted, but it had brought home the fact that he was screwed ten ways to Sunday.

"That sounds...terrifying." She put her hand on her flat stomach, almost as if she was experiencing the same gut-rolling sickness he had.

"You know the thought that went through my head?" With the electrical failure, he hadn't been able to do his damn job, making all his training useless and giving him a split second for the fear to lay a clean punch to his gut. "It occurred to me that everyone on board was going to have someone to miss them when they were gone. Someone to *notice* when they didn't come back. Me? My dad is the closest I've got to anyone who would give a rat's ass, and he's so far out of the country he wouldn't even hear the news for two months."

The moment of silence that followed his words hammered home the fact that he'd probably just given Arianna the best possible reason she'd have to draw up divorce papers after the holiday. He worked in a dangerous job, was gone half the year and—oh, by the way—he couldn't ever tell her where he was going or even what aircraft he manned when he did his gate hours.

Yeah. He was quite a catch.

"If anything had happened to you, I would have noticed. I would have missed you." She blinked twice, her eyes shiny.

"You hadn't seen me in over a decade." He hadn't even really expected her to show for his birthday bash—especially since he'd posted a notice on a social network board at the last minute and invited a ton of people to the Hard Rock.

"But I planned on looking *you* up when *I* turned thirty in November, so I would have found out then and I would have been... I would have missed you."

"Wait a minute." He moved to face her fully. To read the nuances of her expression to be sure he understood her. "You're saying—"

"I knew we'd both be turning thirty this year and I remembered our deal that we'd…consider each other if we made it to the ripe old age of thirty and were still single."

"Holy hell. You'd been thinking about…us." This changed things. Made his task easier—and harder.

Easier because she clearly had some deeper feelings for him somewhere, so maybe she'd hear him out about giving their crazy marriage a try.

Tougher, though, because now they *both* ran the risk of being hurt when things didn't work out. Not that he was a pessimist. But no woman signed on for the kind of life he had to offer—she'd be alone most of the time. And when she was, she'd have no clue whether he was twenty-five miles away or five thousand.

He'd signed on for tougher missions than convincing Arianna Demakis to stay married to him. But the toll of failure was going to hurt a lot worse than any fallout a battle could have delivered.

3

"I'm not sure if I was thinking about *us*." She traced the handle of the stoneware mug with her finger, musing over how much to give away about the torch she'd always carried for him. "But I've definitely thought about you. I knew the marriage pact was a joke when we made it, yet I always had it in the back of my head to check in on you one day and see if you'd followed your dreams. If you were happy."

She lifted her gaze to find him watching her with an avidness that made her...hot. There was no other word for it. Tempted as she was to act on that heat, though, she didn't want to miss an opportunity to talk through their unorthodox predicament. Did he think she was crazy to still wear the wedding ring from a drive-through ceremony? Maybe he'd only arranged this meeting with her to get the ring back and sign the papers that would end the charade.

Her thumb went to the expanse of silver filigree and rubbed the surface. She didn't always wear it on her finger. Sometimes she put it on a chain around her neck so as not to cause too much speculation. She'd worn it one way or another since he'd given it to her, though. Partly, it reminded her of him.

It also reminded her that she'd made a fool of herself by letting herself believe in starry-eyed romance.

"Happy?" He arched an eyebrow like Mr. Spock debating an alien concept. "My work is fulfilling, but I wouldn't say—"

Her cell phone trilled a sharp note.

"Sorry," she murmured, hopping to her feet before that obnoxious ring tone went off again. "I have to crank the volume when I'm working because the pandemonium backstage can be so loud. I have another show running—" She pressed the button to answer. "Hello?"

"Thank God you're home." Krista's voice rushed into her ear. "Your snake handler is a no-show, a handful of the dancers had too much to drink at a Christmas party and the theater manager is ripping Maisey up one side and down the other. I told her to delay the start time by ten minutes but—"

Arianna closed her eyes. "I'm on my way."

"I'm really sorry to call you in. It's just that I thought I'd be giving performers a little encouragement, not taking charge of a whole lot of problems." Krista's voice sounded high and nervous. In the background, lively holiday tunes played over the house speaker system.

"It's okay. See you in ten." Swallowing hard, she disconnected the call and tried to think of how to frame the right apology for ditching an air force captain fresh home from service to his country.

On Christmas.

But Dylan was already on his feet. "Where are we headed?"

SHE FILLED HIM in on the problems during the drive over to the Pompeii Theatre. She hadn't been able to convince him to stay behind, even though she'd urged him to relax and enjoy the tree lights and some cookies she'd made in a fit of holiday domesticity.

"I just feel so bad about doing this on your first night home." Arianna fretted as she handed her keys to the valet at the Pompeii and hurried toward the theater entrance.

With his long strides, Dylan easily kept pace. "We enjoyed the tree for…what? Fifteen minutes?"

Her eyes went to the watch on her wrist. It was after 12:00 a.m. and past time for the *"Midnight" Christmas Circus* to be under way.

He shrugged. "Usually it's *my* work that hauls me away from a good evening, and I can tell you, the reasons for having to fire up a military mobile command center on short notice usually aren't half as entertaining as intoxicated dancers and missing snake handlers."

"I assure you, if Ricardo the Reptile Raiser wants to work in this town again, he will show up for his performance time." Arianna had left messages for the snake charmer at his home and on his cell. She slid a sideways glance at Dylan when he held open the door for her. "Although your point is well taken—I'm glad we're tackling my work problems tonight instead of yours. Ideally, however, we'd be toasting each other with champagne, then…"

She trailed off, only because she wasn't sure what would happen next. Her heart still hurt from the way he'd left her four months ago—and the way he'd never phoned to touch base in the weeks that followed. But that hurt didn't take away the attraction that still zinged between them, even though she knew she'd be an even bigger romantic fool to give in to it.

"Go on," he urged, leaning close to whisper in her ear as they took a wide staircase down to the dressing-room area backstage. "You stopped at the juicy part of that story."

Heat smoked through her veins again, even as she stressed about the show.

"I'm not sure how the story ends, I guess."

"We could take turns making up possible scenarios for what would happen after the champagne," he suggested, nodding to a harried-looking stage manager who was speaking urgently into his headset as he passed them.

The sounds of holiday music swelled, but didn't cover the hum of a restless crowd out front. Having a performance start late was never ideal, even though Vegas audiences were usually easygoing. A midnight Christmas-show crowd wasn't quite as forgiving, however, and Arianna didn't blame them.

Still…Dylan's invitation was a pleasant distraction from the problems she couldn't fix.

"Hmm… If tequila makes us think of marriage, maybe champagne would put us in the mood for…a romantic movie?"

A weak effort at best. She couldn't picture Dylan sitting through some weepy chick flick, even after downing half a magnum.

His arched eyebrow said as much. "We'd better wait and continue this later." He pointed toward a throng of performers talking in raised voices off to one side of a darkened set behind the main stage curtain.

Arianna hastened her pace as Krista broke away from the crowd to join her.

"Still no word from Ricardo. The show girls are in the dressing area guzzling coffee to sober up, but I'm not sure it will help." Krista rattled off the news, efficient but nervous.

Arianna didn't blame her. It sucked being the point person for everyone's problems, yet that was exactly her most important job responsibility.

"They're fired." She raised her voice so all the gathered dancers could hear. She'd made up her mind about this on the drive over. As much as she hated to cut anyone on a holiday, she knew there were twenty other dancers who would give their right ear for the job and who would respect their fellow entertainers enough not to pull stunts like this. "Send out the opening act, we'll come up with a plan for choreography. Everyone else here is a professional and I know they'll pull together to make this work."

Her actions were simple. Her tone clipped. In theory, she could have given the directive to Maisey or Krista over the phone. However, experience taught her that sometimes the fastest way to cool down a tense situation was to send in a big gun. Her physical presence spoke louder than any advice she delivered. Maisey was already snapping orders to the tech guys in the sound booth on her headset while Krista straightened the headpiece on one of the first girls who would take the stage in a set modeled to look like a sleigh.

Even Dylan jumped in to help, offering advice to a stagehand trying to reassemble a part on the gear mechanism that rotated the sets to accommodate fifteen different scenes.

"What about the snake handler?" The theater manager trundled over, his forehead sweaty and his cheeks red. An unpleasant micromanager, Bernard didn't usually allow third-party producers like her to bring in pre-packaged shows such as this one, but his boss had loved Arianna's pitch. So now Bernard had no choice but to roll with it. Would he try to use tonight's crisis to his advantage? Could she trust him to carry out her orders? Normally she would be able to read the situation without hesitation, but her nerves were a wreck and her life was a jumbled mess thanks to her hunky "husband" who stooped a few feet away picking up feathers off the floor.

She forced her shoulders back and her chin up, refusing to let Bernard see the cracks in her professional confidence. "I have a substitute act if necessary."

"Ricardo has been featured in all the show literature—"

"Our contract makes provisions for substitutions when needed." She kept her tone even as her eyes met Dylan's reassuring gray gaze across the open backstage space. The connection she felt to him was a novel experience. She wasn't the kind of woman to let a man fight her battles. Still, the protective vibe emanating from her lover-turned-husband was enough to make even a tough girl's toes curl. "If you'll excuse me, Bernard, I've got some choreography to approve for my dancers. We can't afford any more delays."

He huffed and stomped after her, but the show music was swelling. The crowd out front quieted briefly before applauding as the curtain rose to reveal the first number— a scantily clad Mrs. Claus high kicking her way through the reindeer barn to choose the right fleet-footed coursers for her sleigh ride. The song was sweet and frivolous and rattled through the lower quality speakers that peppered the halls backstage.

"And we're off," she assured herself as she raced down the stairs toward the main dressing area where the choreographer would be filling the holes in the dance routines.

Performers rushed past her, holding their sequined antlers firmly in place for the reindeer number, or soothing anxious dogs on leashes for the "Canine Parade."

"Ms. Demakis," Bernard blustered at her as he hurried to keep up. "I cannot tolerate this sort of unprofessionalism."

"Nor can I." She spun to meet his beady gaze, pausing just outside the makeup room. "I do not enjoy terminating employees on a holiday, but for the sake of the Pompeii and my responsibility to your patrons, I've done just that. If you'll be so kind as to send one of the stagehands down with a walkie, I'll ensure the rest of this performance exceeds your expectations."

His mouth worked silently for a moment, as if he hoped to find some way to argue with her and failed. Thank you, God. She didn't need any more distractions on a night when she should have been sitting under a Christmas tree with one sexy air force captain. She would smooth things over here and then get back to giving Dylan the welcome home he deserved.

"Maybe if you didn't book three shows on top of each

other, this wouldn't have happened," he said finally, crossing his arms over his barrel chest. "With a little more supervision, those girls wouldn't have been downing red apple sangrias before they went on stage."

If there hadn't been a smidge of truth in what he said, she would have been able to brush it aside. As it stood, the criticism stung. She was ambitious—sometimes to a fault.

"I can't change what has already happened," she reminded him, her words stiff and formal, at odds with the lively Christmas jazz still humming through unseen speakers. "Moving forward, do you have a preference for how I should handle things this evening?"

He harrumphed. Shuffled his feet. "Maybe you shouldn't fire the girls on Christmas, is all."

With that, he stomped away, leaving her to her professional responsibilities and her regrets. She was working on Christmas even though she'd been so determined to make Dylan's homecoming special. Worse, she was ready to ax a few dancers only just beginning to find their way in a tough profession.

Midnight Christmas Circus didn't call for a Scrooge character, but if it did, apparently she'd landed the starring role. Was it any wonder she'd latched on to a guy who wouldn't stay in town long enough to see below her well-maintained surface to the mess of the real woman beneath?

ARIANNA PUT ON one hell of a show.

Dylan watched the final set of dancers go out for the grand finale, mesmerized by the contrast between the seamless flow of performers onto the stage and the chaos behind the scenes that lasted from the late start to the madhouse rush to the finish. He stood in the shadows next to the weird snake handler who'd showed up about fifteen minutes before he was scheduled to go on stage.

Ricardo kept his main snake—Sheba—draped over his

shoulders so that the spotted Indian python glared at Dylan with beady eyes. Though nonvenomous, any snake would sure as hell bite when provoked, as Ricardo had shown his audience when he offered his scarred hands for illustration. While Dylan appreciated that the guy hadn't sewn the creature's mouth shut the way some conscienceless street performers had been known to do, Dylan didn't plan on letting Sheba get close enough to test her teeth out on him.

"You are here with our Ari?" Ricardo asked him even though his eyes remained on the dancers waiting nearby for the final curtain call.

"Yes." Dylan hadn't lost sight of her since she'd returned to the main floor after working with the choreographer downstairs.

She'd seemed distracted since then—her expression closed, her posture tense—making him wonder if things had turned ugly with the intoxicated dancers. He understood that had been a tough call for her.

"She does not let anyone close to her," the man offered, patting his snake on the head. "She never socializes with the cast."

Dylan wondered how well the guy could know Arianna when the Christmas circus show was a once-a-year deal. Still, he couldn't deny a flare of jealousy that someone knew Ari better than him.

"A manager has to draw boundaries." The military wouldn't function if the colonels spent their time in team-building exercises with new airmen. Hierarchy was earned and it worked.

Ricardo nodded absently and shifted the python closer to the dancers, sending three of them skittering away, squealing and giggling.

"Just don't forget, the ones who have the most boundaries often put them there because they possess the most fragile hearts." For a moment, he locked eyes with Dylan, as if to telegraph the import of the message.

Making a weird moment even weirder.

Then again, maybe the snake handler wasn't as much of a whack job as Dylan had taken him for.

Dancers started moving past them in a swirl of green sequins and white feathers. Headdresses bobbed past him while the floorboards vibrated with the tap of a hundred red satin high heels. Ricardo followed them out while the applause thundered through the theater. Backstage, assistants and stagehands high-fived each other. Arianna's second-in-command, Maisey, hugged Krista, a big-time recording artist who headlined a lot of Ari's shows.

But the producer herself?

She remained in the shadows, speaking into a walkie-talkie while her eyes roamed over some notes on a clipboard. It wasn't the snake charmer's words in his head that suddenly made him close the distance between them. It was seeing her put herself in the background, the indispensable cog in the wheel of a show that would have never gotten off the ground without her.

"You did it." He slid an arm around her waist and kissed her temple, knowing the clock was ticking on his chances to touch her…unless he could convince her to give their relationship another try. "Congratulations."

"Thank you." She stared out at the stage, though something about her expression suggested she was a million miles away. "But I'm not sure ruining your homecoming was worth it."

The applause continued while the master of ceremonies called out one set of performers after another to take their bows.

"Nothing was ruined." He eased back to look at her, but his hand didn't leave the indent of her waist, his fingers greedy for more of her. "I can guaran-damn-tee you that my life could use a whole lot more festivity, and this night brought me that."

She turned to him, her dark eyes narrowed. "I noticed you talking to Ricardo just now. I can't imagine that conversation proved festive or uplifting." She shuddered. "No doubt it involved waving Sheba under your nose?"

"Well…maybe. But I enjoyed everything else. Mostly, I liked seeing you in your element. I've tried to picture what you do as a producer. Now I know." He drew her back a step to give the exiting performers more room as they hurried toward the dressing rooms. Assistants were already collecting headdresses for storage.

Arianna laughed and handed her clipboard and headset to a stagehand as she and Dylan walked toward the exit.

"This is only a small facet. The tougher work is finding funding for the productions and making all the necessary pieces of the puzzle come together each time. Tonight's work was…"

She bit her lip in a gesture so uncharacteristic of the strong woman he knew that he stopped in his tracks.

"Hey. Everything okay?" He tipped her chin up to see her expression more clearly in the low light.

"Fine." She nodded. "I was going to say my on-site work is like babysitting, but that sort of thinking is exactly what makes people view me as…aloof. I don't mean to be. When I'm here, my job is to oversee the flow of people and events, solving problems as they come up. It's not tough. It's…"

"Management." He understood better than she realized. "And your contributions are a bigger deal than you're letting on. You let yourself retreat to the background here, but you are one of the most vibrant, passionate people I know."

"Me?" She shook her head. "Hardly."

"You are the center of all this." He gestured toward the mass of dancers, performers, musicians, dogs and a few loose white geese. "You make it all happen."

She folded her arms and narrowed her gaze, even though he could see a hint of a smile quirking her lips.

"I'm not conceding the geese add that much to this show," she confided in a teasing tone. "But I guess I know what you mean. Since when did you get so wise, Captain Rivera?"

"All I've done is work for the past decade. If I hadn't learned a few things by now, I'd be mighty disappointed in myself." Laying his hand lightly between her shoulder blades, he pointed toward the exit. "Are you ready to make a break for it and celebrate Christmas at last?"

She checked her slim silver wristwatch, but he already knew the time. It was almost 2:00 a.m. Long past time for him to start romancing his wife if he wanted any shot of keeping her.

"Definitely."

"Would you mind if I drive?" He grabbed her cape where she'd hung it near some folded risers when they'd first entered the theater.

"Sure." She pulled her keys from her purse and handed them to him. "Is this a guy, need-to-be-in-control thing?"

"Actually, nothing turns me on more than seeing you in charge." He dropped the cape onto her shoulders and leaned in close enough to hear her swift intake of breath.

Close enough to catch a hint of the exotic floral scent she applied so lightly he had to really hunt for it to get the full effect. He felt as hypnotized by her as Sheba had been for that damn flute.

"But…?" she prodded, forcing him to remember their conversation. They'd been talking about a plan for tonight. How to celebrate Christmas. He needed to pay attention. Because while getting naked sounded really, really good in the short term, he wasn't convinced red-hot sex alone would keep her from signing divorce papers.

He stepped back, out of the range of her feminine scent and steeled himself to go a little longer without touching her.

"I've got a surprise for you and I'd like to make a quick stop on the way home to give it to you."

"Oh?"

"I'm going to prove to you that that vibrant, passionate person I knew in high school is still very much a part of who you are now."

4

"THE DRIVE-THROUGH wedding chapel?"

Arianna stared out the windshield of her car as Dylan pulled into a parking space outside the twenty-four-hour business located off the Strip. She hadn't ridden past it since that night with him four months ago.

Dylan clicked the ignition off and shifted to face her, his knee bumping the console even in her luxury-size sedan.

"You mentioned that you wished the pictures had turned out better from that night." He reached for her left hand and held it between both of his, the simple gesture stirring memories and emotions. "I thought—before we closed the door on the marriage chapter—we ought to at least have a good photo to remember the night we were impulsive. And recreating our wedding night ought to remind you of the woman I see when I look at you."

His words and warm voice made her heart feel all light and fizzy. But damn it, if he really cared about her, why hadn't he called when he was overseas? Why no word from him until a few weeks ago?

"Recreate the wedding?" She wondered if he simply felt guilty about the marriage and wanted to end on a happier note. "You don't have to do that."

The pictures they had weren't terrible. It's not like the

two of them weren't recognizable, or anything. They were just a bit...candid. She'd been flashing toothy gums in her smile, her hair flying away as if it had somewhere else to be...that sort of thing.

What would it be like to relive that crazy night again? Just seeing the inflatable Mr. and Mrs. Claus out front, dressed in wedding finery and holding hands, made her stomach stir with new butterflies.

"I *want* to do this. Besides, the picture is my Christmas present to you." He gave her one of his rare smiles—more a hitch of the lips than a true smile. "I haven't had much time for shopping these past few months."

The reminder of where he'd been touched her, even if his job had taken him away from her.

"In that case..." She couldn't deny feeling a warm pleasure at his thoughtful surprise. "Thank you."

"There's a catch, though."

"Uh-oh."

"We've got to recreate the whole thing so we've got an authentic experience."

"You don't mean—"

"We do the whole shebang—dress, tux, flowers, convertible with the chauffer. Are you game?"

"Really? Are you sure this is how you want to spend your Christmas?"

"Are you kidding me? No matter what happens from here, you're going to be the hottest wife I'll ever have. Who's going to believe I ever landed you without photo evidence?"

She laughed. This whole night reminded her of when they'd gotten hitched the first time. Her impetuous decisions, the wild circumstances, the warm expression in Dylan's eyes that drew her in and made her want to spend decades in that gray gaze. She considered, watching the red and green lights play over his features as a string of flashing holiday bulbs helped advertise "Fresh Floral Arrangements."

"This is a crazy idea."

"But you'll do it?"

She peered around the empty parking lot, the wedding business even slower at this time of year than some of the other staple Las Vegas industries. "At least we won't have to wait in line."

He leaned in to give her cheek a kiss. The momentary heat made her want to close her eyes and savor the sensation. The man. She fought the urge to touch the place he'd kissed with her fingers.

"Great. Go find a dress and I'll arrange the car and driver."

Twenty minutes later, Arianna emerged from a dressing room in a vintage thirties wedding dress—the same gown she'd rented the first time. Eggshell-white and heavy with beads, the dress had simple lines. A straight skirt and a modest neckline in front but a plunging back that made her feel sexy as she walked. She stood in the foyer of the small building where the chapel sold flowers, photos and accessories to "Make Your Wedding the Memory of a Lifetime!" The lettering on the sign was outlined in pink neon and the "memories"—including being serenaded by an Elvis impersonator or chauffeured through the drive-up window in a pink Cadillac—all came with a price.

"Are you ready, miss?" An attendant in a simple blue dress appeared, blinking bleary eyes even though she produced a bright smile. "I'm Caitlin and I'll show you to the car."

Arianna wondered how many other weddings Caitlin would witness before dawn on Christmas morning.

"I'll do that." Dylan stepped out of the dressing area on the opposite side of the foyer, his black tuxedo fitted and sleek. Narrow lapels and a black bow tie had classic appeal, but not nearly as much as the man himself. He offered her his arm. "Ready to make it official? Again?"

She didn't know quite how to answer since she'd planned just to get through the holidays before dissolving the marriage.

"I thought we were just here for the picture?"

"The camera isn't going to capture the romance if we're worrying over divorce papers." He took her hand and looped it under his elbow so that her palm rested on his forearm. The perfect prom-escort walk. "What were you thinking about the first time we did this?"

Caitlin handed Arianna her bouquet—eggshell white roses mixed with a few pale pink ones. A gorgeous, old-fashioned bouquet that worked well with the dress. She dipped her nose to inhale the fragrance, the soft petals a delicate caress on her cheek.

"What was on my mind?" She smiled, remembering that hot summer night with Dylan. The way she'd sneaked into the men's dressing area once she was sure he was alone in there. "Hmm…I remember thinking I couldn't wait to undress you." She lowered her voice when she said it, but she guessed that Caitlin's sudden coughing fit meant their wedding consultant had overheard.

His arm tensed beneath her touch, his muscles flexing. Heat leaped between them as his eyes met hers. His gaze dipped briefly to her mouth and back up to her eyes. Her mouth went dry. The rhythm of her heart stumbled and sped up.

"That's right." He snapped his fingers, eyes coming alive with a naughty gleam. "I forgot a key part of how this all shook down, didn't I?"

He wouldn't. "You don't mean—"

"Caitlin, will you tell the driver we'll be out in just a minute? There's a floral trellis I want to show Arianna that we might want in the photos."

Dylan's hand tightened around her arm as he drew her back toward the floral display and deeper into the building.

"I think the driver is ready—" Caitlin began.

"We won't take long." He held up a single finger as if to

ask for one more moment. Then, his cheek brushed against Arianna's hair as he leaned close to whisper, "Come on."

He slid an arm around her waist and propelled her with him toward the floral display. Another day, there might be more workers in the chapel to show them dresses and flowers, but now the bright interior was quiet except for the sound system piping in nonstop holiday carols.

"She's going to follow us," Arianna worried aloud, her eyes only vaguely taking in the Christmas bouquets of poinsettias and holly branches mingled with snow-white roses.

"Not fast enough, though." Dylan tugged her between a narrow walkway of trellises and vine-covered arbors. When they reached the end of the row, he turned her to face him.

They stood, one fast-beating heart to another, and she imagined she wore the same mischievous smile that he did.

"I'm glad you said yes." His words scratched a husky note, echoing another night.

No matter how much she'd like to blame the tequila that had kicked off his birthday celebration, she'd known exactly what she was doing that night. She'd just had a few less inhibitions.

Now, the past and the present blended until it didn't matter if they were reliving the old moment or creating a new one. Her hands landed on the front of his tuxedo, the same kind he'd worn the first time since he hadn't been carrying around his dress blues when they'd tied the knot.

She would have said yes even if he'd been wearing Bermuda shorts and a Hawaiian shirt.

"Me, too." Her thin scrap of voice barely made a sound in the still air between them. She held her breath.

Hoped.

One of his hands cupped her cheek while the other slid around her waist, drawing her close. The beads on her dress poked through the fabric to abrade her skin, but the warmth of Dylan on the other end of that touch made the sensation very, very pleasurable.

His mouth brushed hers with a tenderness that set this kiss apart from any other they'd shared. Gently, he nipped the fullness of her sensitive lower lip, drawing it between his. She all but melted against him, the combination of his heat and scent, his male strength and his obvious desire making her weak in the knees. She fisted his lapels between her fingers, wishing she could hold on to the moment half so fiercely.

The fragrance of freesia and pine boughs mingled with the scent of Dylan's faded aftershave—spicy and male. She could have breathed it in forever as his tongue stirred a longing in her veins and a deep hunger that could only be satisfied by this man and his strong, capable body.

A discreet cough warned them they weren't alone.

"Captain and Mrs. Rivera?" a feminine voice intruded on Arianna's sensual imaginings, calling her back to the moment. "We ask that our couples focus on the ceremony in order to respect our other patrons' time."

Dylan broke away from Arianna, her lips cooling fast without his to warm them. He tucked her close and called out to Caitlin, who remained discreetly out of view.

"We'll be right there." He smoothed Arianna's hair away from her face and glanced at her dress before straightening the skirt along her right hip. "I just didn't want to jinx the whole thing by skipping that part," he confided for her ears only.

She was still shaky from the kiss and the powerful need pumping through her. She'd missed Dylan, but she hadn't realized how much and how deeply until that kiss.

"You definitely did the past justice." Her voice sounded strange to her ears. She hardly recognized that breathy timbre. "I remember being wound tight by the time we said the vows."

They'd barely made it back to his hotel, clothes coming off in the elevator.

"The same goes for me now." His eyes locked on hers, his hands still on her waist.

"What were we thinking?" She didn't want to ruin the moment, but she'd never stopped wondering what had gotten them to the wedding chapel. "What made two smart, thirty-year-old overachievers say to hell with everything and make the most romantic commitment—one that should be so meaningful—on a whim?"

Caitlin cleared her throat on the other side of an arbor covered in artificial orange blossoms. "I'd be happy to show you some more arrangements."

"We've decided we have enough flowers," Dylan barked back, his eyes never leaving Arianna. "We're just trying to make sure we go into the sacred state of matrimony with our heads on straight, so we'd like another minute."

"Oh. Er. Of course." Their wedding consultant started to walk away, judging by the tap of shoes across tile. "I'll just be right outside if you need anything. Don't forget, Santa ends his shift in twenty minutes, so if you'd like photos with him, we should take those soon."

"Got it," Dylan called to her, making no move to follow the woman anywhere.

"It's okay," Arianna protested, not wanting to put too much emphasis on that night. She picked at a perfect pink petal in her bouquet until it loosened and fell free. "We can get going. I've just wondered about it sometimes."

"Me, too. And you want to know what I think?" He spoke reasonably, as if they were back in high school debating the merits of one video game system over another.

"Yes. Please." She appreciated that he hadn't just breezed into town and picked up right where they left off, as enjoyable as that might have been in the short term. He didn't try to seduce her with his kisses. Instead, he analyzed the passion and helped her find the source.

Because what she felt for Dylan and what had happened between them had sent her life into a tailspin.

"I think we're both so damn hardworking and ambitious that we've put off personal needs for a helluva long time. But when that birthday rolled around…we remembered how great it feels to trust somebody. To connect with someone who really knows you."

"How well could we have known each other when we hadn't been together in so long?"

His hands flattened against her rib cage, smoothing a short, heated path up her sides.

"The years don't matter. The connection was there. Is there."

He sounded so certain it made her want to believe him. Except if that was true…

"Is it wrong to repeat the vows when…you know. We're not even sure they're going to last the week, let alone a lifetime?" She hadn't thought it through that far before, but now that she stood in her wedding gown next to Dylan— again—the ethics of the situation were definitely coming back to bite her.

"We're not repeating the legal part of the ceremony," Dylan assured her. "I just paid for all the stuff we'd need to recreate the photos."

A curious mixture of relief and disappointment curled through. "Oh. Okay."

"Did I mention you look incredibly beautiful?"

Her heartbeat kicked up again, the tone of his voice affecting her like a caress. She wasn't going to think about the future beyond today. Christmas day.

Her second-chance wedding with Dylan.

She might be a romantic fool, but no matter what else it might mean, she was definitely going to have a second honeymoon night. And that alone was going to keep her smiling as if she'd just opened the best present ever.

"THANK YOU FOR the photos," Arianna said to Dylan as she scrolled through the images on her cell phone.

They'd finished up the pictures relatively quickly once they'd left their floral hideaway. They hadn't held up any other weddings since business was slow at the chapel on Christmas. Now, back in their own clothes, they strode through the lobby of Ari's building shortly before dawn, Dylan enjoyed watching the play of expressions on her face as she viewed each new image. For a few extra bucks, he'd dispensed with the fancy formal packages and just had the pictures emailed to her.

"They turned out better than the first ones?" He looked over her shoulder as they stepped inside the elevator. "That was another reason we got this batch of pictures so fast— the photographer felt bad we weren't happy with the first photos."

"He made up for it." She smiled as she pointed toward one of them kissing in the back of the convertible. The way her bouquet rested in her hand made the roses a border along the bottom of the frame, her dark features a gorgeous contrast to the pale flowers.

"You look incredible." He'd wanted the wedding redo to get Arianna thinking romantic thoughts, even though he'd believed the first round of wedding pictures were great.

He kept a copy of one of them on his phone. They were both smiling like fiends. He'd pulled up that picture a couple hundred times since he'd seen her last.

So yeah, he'd done the photo thing for her. But he hadn't anticipated the way it would affect him, too. He'd missed her for months, wanted her for years. Now, he finally had her—if he could keep her. He couldn't make a mistake.

"Me?" she scoffed as she jabbed the button for the thirty-eighth floor. "You look ready for your close-up on some Hollywood red carpet. George Clooney never wore a suit so well."

The cabin lifted them swiftly and he slid an arm around her waist—pure instinct—to keep her steady. He felt her quick intake of breath and her reaction ratcheted up his own.

"We can finish the story now," he reminded her. "Figure out what happens after the champagne toast under the Christmas tree."

She thumbed off the screen of her phone and dropped it back into her purse.

"Maybe we drag the blankets out onto the floor of the living room," she suggested, walking her fingers up his chest in a suggestive dance.

The light touch was magnified a hundredfold because of the months they'd spent apart.

"Do you really think you'll have the blankets out before I get your clothes off?"

He felt her shiver and would have said more, but the elevator stopped on the thirtieth floor. He swallowed back the urge to snarl at whoever had halted their progress to her condo, and wasn't surprised when a couple of obviously intoxicated twentysomethings stood wavering in the hallway when the elevator doors opened. They smelled like a brewery and looked like they'd been dragged through one backward.

"Dude." The one guy—wearing a ball cap with a suit jacket and jeans—shook his head in a confused daze. "You going down?"

Dylan pressed the button to close the doors. "Sorry, man. Going up."

"Not fast enough," Arianna whispered just as the doors closed, giving them privacy again.

Her dark hair tumbled over her shoulders in a sweep of thick waves even though she'd pinned the front back with pearl combs for the wedding photos. He reached for the combs now and loosened first one, then the other. Her hair was so full it almost obscured her face.

"I think it's your turn," he reminded her. "I just took your clothes off in the 'what happens under the tree' game."

"You're assuming you'd catch me long enough to get my clothes off," she teased, then stepped back to do a little shimmy. "I might decide to show you some of my best showgirl moves first."

"You'd put all your dancers to shame." He gestured her out of the cabin ahead of him when the elevator stopped at her floor, but she grabbed the front of his flight suit with her hands and drew him with her. She walked backward, tugging him forward.

"I'm not so sure about that, but I've learned some tricks over the years that I've been watching them." She reached in her purse and halted. "You still have my keys, right?"

He was already pulling them out of his pocket. "Affirmative. Nothing's slowing us down now unless you want it to."

"Are you kidding?" She arched up on her toes and kiss-licked a spot just beneath his jaw. "I've had a highlight reel of our 'best of' moments going through my head for four months. I wouldn't mind recreating a few of those as thoroughly as we redid the photos."

Heat blasted over his skin as he realized she'd savored every minute of that night, too. He hadn't had as much to drink as she might believe, considering they'd gotten married on impulse. So he'd been fully cognizant of every second of their wedding night. Had she been as clearheaded as him? He'd thought it often enough that night. Wanted to believe it now since it would mean she'd gone into that wedding chapel with more than just a tequila buzz driving her vows.

"I remember that night perfectly." He wanted her to know that ceremony hadn't been an accident. Definitely hadn't been a mistake.

She took the keys from him with hands that trembled a

little. He breathed in the scent of her perfume mingled with the fragrance of her shampoo. He wanted her so badly his teeth ached. Honest to God, ached from it.

"Me, too," she admitted softly while she turned the key in the lock, not looking at him.

The confession blew him away.

Part of him wanted to stop this sizzling heat between them long enough to discuss the implications of what they'd just said. But it was past the time for talking. After so long without her, he'd told her the truth when he'd said he couldn't stop for anything unless she put the brakes on this.

He'd been hanging on to his control by a thread all through those damn photos.

As she pushed open the door, he took the weight of it from her and held it for her. When they were both inside the cinnamon-scented condo, he bolted the lock.

"I'd better get that champagne now if we have any hope of a toast tonight." She let her purse slide off her shoulder and tossed her cape on a bar stool.

Or at least she tried to toss it aside. She was shaking and breathing hard, so her throw missed the chair and the light wrap slid to the floor.

"Maybe I'll unzip your skirt with my teeth before you make it to the fridge."

She froze in midmotion, her body moving toward the refrigerator and then—stopping. She halted awkwardly, her arm already raised toward the stainless-steel double doors on the kitchen appliance.

In a heartbeat, he was in front of her, breathing her air as she exhaled a shaky puff.

"Not sure I can top that one," she confessed, her voice a thready whisper.

His pulse thrummed harder. Hotter. Until all he could think about was being inside her.

"That's perfect, because I'm done playing games."

5

His lips met hers and not a moment too soon.

Arianna had been dying for the feel of his lips on hers ever since the dizzying preview he'd given her back at the wedding chapel. Now, she received the kiss with as much finesse as a dieting woman scarfing a forbidden bit of chocolate.

Her arms went around his neck, pulling him closer, while his hands molded her hips to his, as if they could somehow consummate this thing without getting their clothes off.

"My God, I've missed you." He spoke the words into her skin as he kissed his way along her cheek and down into the sensitive hollow of her neck. The sound vibrated along her nerve endings and made her shiver with want.

"I've missed you, too." She combed her hands along his shoulders and down his chest to the zipper of his flight suit. She raked it south to expose his T-shirt. The skin-warmed cotton was sexier than silk sheets.

But his urgency turned her on like nothing else.

His hands found the buttons for her lace blouse and twisted them until he'd unfastened each one. Her necklace fell in a heavy skid of beads down the front of her, landing on the kitchen tiles. He walked her backward, skimming the sheer blouse off her shoulders and sliding his hands over her silk camisole, tugging down the straps so he could nip his way along her collarbone.

Sensations chased through her, one after the other, until her body all but vibrated with alternating shivers and flashes of heat. She arched and wriggled, helping him with her clothes until she wore nothing but a sheer, white bra and her red skirt. They had kissed and undressed their way to the living room, with Dylan losing only his shoes. His half-discarded flight suit clung to narrow hips and a damn fine butt.

He edged away to look at her, his gaze roaming the curve of small breasts that didn't require much support. They weren't showy, but Dylan didn't seem to mind, plus the delicate size allowed her to wear extravagant Italian lingerie without concern for function.

"You like?" She teased, nudging one strap down her arm to start the slow slide of see-through lace down her left breast.

Dylan's feral growl rumbled through her a second before he latched on to one tight peak, drawing hard on the taut nipple until her knees turned to liquid.

She fell into him, supporting herself by locking onto his broad biceps. Pleasure smoked through her at the feel of him against her. He was hard everywhere and she wanted nothing more than to mold herself to fit.

"I need to undress you." She tugged ineffectually at the flight suit, her attention distracted by the ribbons of desire spiraling out from where his mouth fixed on her breast.

It had been so long. Way too freaking long.

"Amen to that." He worked the front clasp of her bra and freed her from the skimpy lace, making it easy for her to shed it.

She reached for the waistband of her skirt, ready to ditch that, too, but he lightly restrained her hands.

"Let me." His eyes were fixed on her body for a long moment before they lifted to meet her gaze. "Okay?"

She nodded jerkily, fine with anything he wanted to do as long as he did it *soon*. Her heart raced so fast she was lightheaded. Her extremities tingled. Her lips trembled.

He shucked his flight suit and raked his T-shirt up and over his shoulders, all while studying her body like a puzzle that required solving. Seriously? She already had a very good idea what to do with all the he-man action tenting his boxers.

"Don't overanalyze this," she warned. "Anything you do, I'm going to really like."

"It doesn't hurt to maximize your potential for pleasure." A flash of teeth was all she got for a smile. "Would you mind turning around?"

Her mouth went dry.

She turned, her stocking feet pivoting easily on the stretch of Persian carpet near the sofa. Her hair shifted against her skin, the feel of the strands a silky tease for the touches she *really* craved.

Then his hands were bracketing her hips, holding her steady. His body brushed hers as he came up behind her, the hard length of his erection nudging her. She swayed forward until her hands found the back of the sectional, her fingers digging into the supple leather.

He swept aside her long hair with his fingers. Bent over her so that his lips grazed the back of her neck near the curve of her shoulder. Moisture pooled between her thighs. Her nipples beaded to painful tightness. Every part of her wanted his touch. His kiss.

She closed her eyes and focused on the sensations, losing herself in the feel of his lips gliding down her spine. She arched into him, seeking a firmer touch, but he grazed one light nip after another in a path along her vertebrae that led to her skirt.

And found the zipper with his teeth.

She remembered his promise of what he'd do to her, his sensual threat to undress her this way. She was so keyed up that it seemed as if every hitch of the zipper teeth parting stoked her higher. The warmth of Dylan's breath heated her skin as he parted the wool fabric. Revealed the barest hint of white thong that she'd worn precisely because she'd known she would be seeing him tonight.

When he reached the base of the zipper, he paused. Cinched the fabric down her hips with his hands until the skirt slid to the floor.

She waited, breathing in the cinnamon-scented air, all her senses heightened. Ready.

Then, rising to his feet, he bent over her, his chest pressed to her back, his hand coming around to palm the heat between her legs. She nearly flew apart. Would have done just that if he'd moved his fingers against her at all. But he just cupped the damp heat of her panties, pinning her body to his so she could feel every inch of his erection along her bottom. Waiting for her.

"Please," she murmured.

"I'm going to make you come first." He spoke directly into her ear, right at the same moment he moved his fingers in a circle around her sex.

She cried out, the sensations sending a lightning bolt through her veins. She teetered on the precipice…so deliciously close she wasn't sure she wanted to tip the rest of the way over. Yet she couldn't stop herself.

"I'm so close. So, so—"

He slid aside the thong and touched her, homing in on the slick heat until the sensations overwhelmed her. She came hard, crumpling in his arms and reaching mindlessly over her shoulder to touch him, any part of him. She found his stubbled jaw with her palm and rested her hand there while wave after wave of lush pleasure undulated over her body.

Faint aftershocks continued to rock her while Dylan shifted their few remaining clothes and—she could tell by his movements—rolled on a condom. He entered her inch by slow, amazing inch. Lights flashed behind her eyes, her body still in the grip of incredible release. Now, her feminine muscles pulsed around him lightly. Intermittently.

Yet she could tell he felt it by the way he stopped each time, his whole body tensing. She tried to be patient, to wait for him since she knew he wanted to make this last. But it had been forever since they'd been together and her body seemed to have a will independent of her brain....

"Wait." He must have read her mind since he caught her hips with his hands before she could dictate the pace.

She straightened so that she stood close to him, his chest hot against her back.

"I can't. The feel of this…" She couldn't describe it. "I can't wait."

"I'm not going anywhere. Not anytime soon."

But he would eventually. The clarification made a warning light go off—albeit very quietly—in the back of her mind. Dylan wasn't going to stay with her forever, no matter what the vows said. His job would have him on the other side of the world. And she worked on Christmas. All the reasons they hadn't gotten together as teenagers still applied.

"Arianna." His voice softened with a note she'd never heard before, a gentle coaxing that felt unique to her name. "Stay with me."

How had he sensed that she'd let her fears creep in?

"Don't read my mind," she warned him, sighing with greedy satisfaction as he pushed fully inside her.

He chuckled as he kissed his way down her neck and over her bare shoulder, brushing aside her hair and giving her goose bumps from his light touches.

"I'm going to take you to bed now." He spoke against her skin, the words a gentle vibration along her flesh.

Her heart caught at the idea of them together...in her bed. She'd never sleep in it again without thinking of him. Then again, she'd never see this couch the same way now that she'd sprawled over the back of it to accommodate him....

It was a surprise when he withdrew from her, even though she'd had a warning. He draped a chenille throw blanket around her shoulders and tucked her close to his side, leading her unerringly to the bedroom even though he'd never been in it before. A strand of red and white Christmas lights adorned the huge wooden headboard of the sleigh bed, a frivolous touch in a room that hadn't otherwise been decorated except for a few bird ornaments on the windowsill.

The rising sun hadn't penetrated the plantation shutters on the smaller windows, at least, not yet.

He tugged back the covers to reveal simple white sheets, the quiet intimacy of the act making her feel...bound to him. By him.

It wasn't all together unpleasant.

He began kissing her then and she forgot to worry about what was happening between them. She just let it happen. He kissed her senseless, laid her on the bed and stretched out over her. Nudging her thighs wide, he made room for himself there. This time, when he came inside her, his gray eyes were locked on hers.

What did this perceptive man see when he looked at her?

Taking the coward's way out, she closed her eyes and locked her legs around his hips. She knew what she wanted. Knew what they both needed.

For now, it would be enough.

Dylan propped himself over her with his arms, taking his own weight while she moved against him. The spicy male musk of his skin enticed her to put her nose to his jaw and take a taste.

More memories of the last time they'd been together. The ways she'd let go of her inhibitions and just…felt. Maybe Dylan remembered that, too, because the guttural noise he made rumbled right through her. She blinked her eyes open to find him pinning her with eyes the shade of molten steel.

She couldn't look away.

Wrapping her arms around his neck, she held on tight as he found a rhythm that drove them both to the edge. The thrust of his hips called forth gasps of pleasure from her lips, her breath coming in thick pants.

Beads of sweat broke out along his forehead as he held back and held back. He touched her sex with his fingers, nipped her earlobe, whispered sweet things about how much she turned him on….

Then, another orgasm washed through her, the squeeze and thrum of it so strong she'd never guess she'd had one only minutes before. She clung to Dylan, locking onto him in every way possible, her port in a storm of sensations unlike anything she'd ever weathered.

The man turned her inside out.

When his release came, his whole body tensed and tightened, the force of it making her toes curl and her feminine instincts hum with happiness. She kissed him mindlessly wherever she could reach. His neck. Jaw. Shoulder.

Joyful endorphins circled her like the robins that tweeted around characters in old cartoons. Yes. She felt that silly-happy.

Long moments passed as he collapsed beside her and she hung on to those feelings with both hands. She wanted to bask in their amazing chemistry. In the total sense of physical completion.

So she was unprepared for Dylan's soft, sleepy words.

"Merry Christmas, my wife."

HE HAD NO IDEA what time it was when he opened his eyes, head digging deeper into the pillow. The sun slanted through the plantation shutters in Ari's bedroom now, too strong for the closed slats to keep it out fully. But where was she?

He felt her empty pillow, her side of the bed cold. He stared up at the red and white Christmas lights that blinked on her headboard and wondered how she'd reacted to his words as he'd fallen asleep moments after they'd…made love.

There was no doubt that's what had happened for him. But with Ari already out of bed, she obviously wasn't thinking the same thing. For all her joking that he could read her mind, he could never be sure what was running through her head. He'd gotten adept at guessing her moods in high school, mostly because he could never take his eyes off her. Amazingly, some of her habits and gestures remained exactly as he remembered them, so he could make lucky guesses now and then.

But as for how she felt about him and this marriage?

Her absence spoke volumes.

His gut knotted. He didn't have enough time to win her over. Would never have enough time to romance her the way she deserved. His job demanded commitment, extra hours and a hell of a lot of secrecy.

Resentment tightened into a cold fist, something he rarely equated with his job. Shoving aside the covers, he discovered his bag at the end of the bed. A cue to him to get moving? Hopefully just a thoughtful gesture.

He showered and brushed his teeth in a blink, more than ready to find out where things stood with Arianna. To push for more time to explore where this connection might lead.

He wasn't one bit prepared for what he saw.

His strong, power broker lover—the woman who delivered the glitz to Vegas and made it look easy—sat sobbing beneath the Christmas tree. She clutched a wrapped gift in her hands, her tears obvious even from across the room.

"Ari?" He went to her, kneeling beside her.

Her thick hair was still damp from the shower, the waves even longer when wet. The shoulders of her white silk robe were soaked through from her hair while her face was wet with tears. She cried noiselessly, her shoulders shaking in a way that freaked him out.

"What is it? Everything okay?" He pried the small white package with a red bow from her hands and set it aside before gathering her in his arms. Settling her half on his lap.

She shook her head. "Everything is not okay." Tugging tissues from the pocket of her robe, she wiped her eyes. "In my business, we have to go on stage and make everything look good, even when it's not. But this is real life, and I can't put on a happy face when…"

"When what?" He must have missed something. How had they gone from the kind of sizzling encounter they'd had a few hours ago to…this? "I know I probably shouldn't have fallen asleep but I'd been up for thirty-six hours and—"

"It's not you!" she protested, thunking her head twice against his shoulder before she straightened. Sniffled. "It's me. I suck and you deserved a better wife for four months than the one you got stuck with."

He brought her face up so she looked at him. "Do you see me complaining? Last I checked I was shouting to the ceiling that you were the hottest thing on earth."

She laughed, a wry sound that didn't contain half enough humor.

"We both know that's not enough for me to pass myself off as a good wife."

She cared about being a good wife? About pleasing him?

"First of all, we've haven't even spent twenty-four hours together as a married couple, so you should probably cut yourself some slack." He smoothed a wet lock of hair away from her face, imagining how often he would repeat that gesture in a lifetime—if he could figure out what was holding her back from giving him a real chance. "Second, you've made a huge success of everything you've ever undertaken, Ari. Marriage wouldn't be any different."

She sniffed again. "Hypothetically."

"Right. But now that we've gotten over that first crazy lust of a homecoming, we can afford to think less hypothetically." He hadn't wanted to approach it so bluntly, but she seemed so upset, he couldn't put it off any longer. "We married for a reason, and neither of us had enough to drink to sway our judgment all that much. So what if we gave our impulses a little credit and considered…staying together?"

Her breath caught. She put her hand over her lips. For a second, he believed she might smile. But in the end, it was a sob she couldn't hold back. She had to clamp it down with her fingers while she shook her head. Wordlessly, she handed him the wrapped gift she'd been holding when he first came in.

He had a bad feeling.

"What's this?"

"Just open it and you'll…see."

With that ominous invitation still ringing in his ears, he ripped off the ribbon and tore through the paper. If she was going to call the whole thing off, better to find out now and walk out of here before he dug a hole any deeper, right?

He'd always known she wouldn't settle for a guy who was gone most of the time. A simple military man didn't fit in her glitzy world. He opened the box to find a small bottle of Jose Cuervo and a very expensive fountain pen.

"They're not the most personal gifts, but then again, I'm not sure that they're worth crying over." He held the tequila up to the light, remembering the glasses they'd downed the night of his birthday.

"I thought you would find it funny, I guess. We could drink a toast to the past while we signed…you know. The papers." Her voice wavered on the words, but her eyes were clear. Her shoulders steady after the outpouring of emotions earlier. "When you left here so awkwardly last time—as if you couldn't leave fast enough—I feared the wedding was all a joke. A silly fantasy I'd been able to live for a while but was over. And then when you didn't call so we could at least talk about it…"

She trailed off awkwardly. And those softly spoken words full of disappointment hurt him far more than any gag gift. To think of her here—hoping he'd get in touch with her when he couldn't—tore him up. And worse, there wasn't a thing he could do about it.

"My job is restrictive." He'd tried unsuccessfully to explain this to girlfriends in the past. But never to anyone as important as Arianna.

"I remember that." She nodded. Accepting. "But Krista's husband works in the air force and they talk on Skype… all the time. She doesn't always know where he is, but they talk. So when I didn't hear from you until recently—and even then, just enough to say you'd be in town for the holidays…" She cleared her throat and straightened up the ripped wrapping paper he'd left on the floor. "I assumed you were only stopping by to correct a past mistake."

"I don't have the same kind of job as Krista's husband." He keyed in on that since he hadn't heard much of what she said beyond that. The arrow of all the ways he couldn't fulfill her stuck in his chest and made it tough to think about anything else. He'd never been a man of many words, but he'd always thought she understood him. At least, she used to.

Vaguely, he realized she must be nervous since her hands wouldn't be still. It had been a long time since he'd seen her be nervous. He'd sure as hell never seen her as upset as he'd made her this morning.

He'd done that. He'd been responsible for all those tears by never being here and never getting in touch with her.

"You can see why I thought you didn't want to be married," she said quietly, filling the silence since he didn't know how to.

"I can." He couldn't do this to her. Couldn't hurt her any more than he already had. "I've always understood my job would be tough on relationships. I understood it back in high school when I told you my plans. Even then, I didn't want to hold you back from your dreams by asking you to—"

Her eyes went wide. She'd had no clue that he'd loved her forever. Had tried to forget her for her own good.

She watched him expectantly, waiting for declarations he couldn't make and promises he couldn't give. He didn't blame her, but this day was killing him. He took a deep breath.

And made the tough decision.

"I'm going to take a rain check on the tequila toast," he said finally, keeping his voice light. Easy. He tucked the small bottle in the breast pocket of an old gray button-down he'd put on this morning. "But I'm going to put the bottle with the old wedding pictures, which I happen to like." Standing, he strode over to the coffee table where they'd left the original prints scattered the night before. "It'll be a testament to a crazy dream that didn't quite work out. When you're ready to sign the papers that will make things less awkward, just give me a call."

He'd brought his bag out into the front room after his earlier shower, so it wasn't difficult to gather his things. He'd always been more of a tech guy—never good at the emotional stuff. It wasn't fair to expect Arianna to understand him, even if she came a hell of a lot closer than anyone else ever had. He took one last look at his hot wife—the woman of his dreams—with her Christmas tree behind her and the city of Las Vegas spread out in the background beyond the windows. This life—this woman—would never be for him.

Without one thing to recommend himself to her and with no excuse for his sorry-ass lack of commitment to her, thanks to the bigger needs of the job, he headed for the door.

6

"You wait just one minute," Arianna called, seeing the best thing—the best someone—that had ever happened to her walk away. "Dylan Rivera, I'm talking to you, damn it."

On her feet in a flash, she streaked past him to plaster herself between him and the door. Heart beating fast, she grabbed either side of the door frame. Probably a little too dramatic since Dylan didn't seem like the kind of guy to nudge her aside.

But he seemed intent on catching her off guard in every way possible today.

He halted in his tracks. His expression gave nothing away, his eyes unreadable. Neutral. His jaw flexed, though. A sign of annoyance? Frustration?

Too. Damn. Bad. She realized he was right about one thing; she was a passionate person who acted quickly and decisively. That night, she hadn't been some romantic fool she didn't recognize—she'd been herself. The person who loved Dylan Rivera. So she was getting answers from him if she had to shake them loose with her bare hands.

"I'm a private person," she reminded him. "A strong person, maybe. But private. And sensitive. Even so, I bared my soul to you in a flood of tears just now, so I would appreciate it if you could let me talk through—think through—

what's happening here before we make a huge mistake by ignoring this once-in-a-lifetime chemistry we share."

"I'm listening." He made no move to set his bag down. Then again, he hadn't plucked her from the door and made a run for it.

She risked lowering her arms, yet resisted the urge to flatten her palms to his warm chest. When she touched him, she couldn't think straight. And right now, more than anything, she needed to keep her head in order. She needed to find a way past Dylan's barrier so she would know once and for all where they stood as a couple, even if finding out broke her heart. Her feelings for him were well worth any risk.

"You've never made your job clear to me, but I remember that you hoped to work with the most highly classified, coolest military technology in the world." She folded her arms, trying to put the pieces of the Dylan Rivera puzzle together. She was a smart woman, right? She could figure him out, figure *them* out. "I'm going to assume that you achieved those career goals beyond your wildest imaginings and that you're now doing work that limits what you can tell me."

As soon as she said the words aloud, she realized where a military techno-geek stationed in southern Nevada probably worked. She crossed Nellis AFB off the list and wondered why she hadn't considered another scenario before. The Groom Lake facility—more commonly known as Area 51—was so close but supremely well guarded. Her gaze flew to Dylan's face and he quirked an eyebrow.

She scowled at him. "Okay, so maybe I should have put that together sooner, but I've been too busy thinking about why we got married in the first place and if you really *wanted* to be married."

Finally, he set his bag down on the foyer floor. "I wouldn't have married you if I didn't love you to distraction."

"Oh." She reached for her heart, feeling the impact of his statement in a mixture of pain and sweetness. Pain because she'd almost let him walk away when he felt this way about her. Sweetness because…thank God, she hadn't let him walk away. "You should have said something."

"The State of Nevada has it on record, Ari." He took a step closer, his eyes shifting to a softer shade of gray— the familiar eyes of the Dylan she'd known since they first faced each other across a chess board in high school.

She flung her arms around his waist. Buried her head in his shoulder. "I was afraid that was just an effect of the tequila and Vegas."

She held him tight, convincing herself she hadn't dreamed the love words he'd said. He smelled so good. Felt even better.

"God, Ari, I've wanted to be with you since prom night, but it seemed wrong to start something then when we both had big dreams that would consume most of our time and personal devotion." He gripped her shoulders and eased her far enough away to meet her gaze. "I'm so proud of you and everything you've achieved. You amaze me."

"I wish I could see you work," she confessed, so proud of the man he'd grown into she could just burst. "I'll bet you're pretty amazing, too."

He didn't confirm or deny it, but of course, he didn't need to. He'd been brilliant in high school—graduating at the top of their class and going on to the Air Force Academy. When she thought back on their prom night and those milk shakes, she remembered him laying out his dreams for her.

Except…he hadn't been just dreaming. He'd gone on to do all those things he'd confided to her.

"Aside from my feelings for you, Arianna, I let myself envision that you might be the only woman able to handle the crap toll that my job takes on a relationship." His dark brows formed a flat line, concern etched in his gray eyes.

"When we talked at the Hard Rock on my birthday and I started to understand how successful you've become and how much you enjoy your work, I realized you're very independent and that you like it that way. So maybe you'd be okay with a husband who was gone all the time."

"I am, I would. But how could you ever imagine I wouldn't want to hear from you? To know you're okay? Being independent doesn't mean I don't have feelings. You have to give me something to hold on to." She shook her head and dragged him back into her living room, back to the sofa where they'd made love the night before. Being there—beside the tree—helped her feel like a family.

"I never guessed that you were analyzing things so carefully. I figured it was just the hot attraction talking."

"Don't get me wrong. I was dying to have you."

"But while I was sneaking into your dressing room to get a peek at you naked, you were thinking about how we could make a real marriage."

She bit her bottom lip, not denying that her heart had been traveling that path. But she still needed to hear him say he wanted to go that route with her. Loving someone didn't automatically include a life together. She'd seen that often enough.

He shifted on the sofa beside her, the leather creaking. "What I still don't know is what *you* think about us having a real marriage." His gaze wandered over her, as if he could find the answer if he studied her long enough.

Damn it, for all that she'd accused him of not communicating with *her,* he was doing a better job of it than she was.

"I love you," she told him simply, wanting her feelings to be as clear as day. No guessing. "I've worn this wedding band either around my neck or on my finger every single day since you gave it to me four months ago. The only reason I got you the tequila and the pen for Christmas is because I thought you didn't really want to be married. I hoped that if I tried to play it cool, I would be able to pass off the night as just some wild and crazy impulse and we would be able to stay in each other's lives. I didn't want to risk losing you altogether."

"I gave you that ring for you to keep forever." He folded her hands in his and squeezed them gently. Then, he placed his thumb and forefinger on the simple silver band and gave it a small twist. "Nothing would make me happier than to know you'll be wearing it for at least that long. And I promise to try and call you from some windowless room somewhere."

Happy relief soothed the frayed nerves of the morning and the tense weeks when he'd been deployed. Hope and joy swelled in her heart until she felt so full of it that it threatened to spill over onto everything she touched. So finally, she let herself touch him. She pressed her hands to his chest, reveling in the racing beat of his heart that told her he was every bit as emotional about building a future together. She just hoped she could give him the wonderful reassurance he'd given her.

"You were right about me enjoying my job. I will miss you when you're not in town, but I'll definitely keep busy." Now that she wasn't worried he wanted to sign divorce papers, her brain began working through all the ways a marriage could work. "I have a good network of friends."

"I think Ricardo the snake charmer is a little in love with you," Dylan observed, wry humor in his voice.

She shook her head. "You don't have to worry about Ricardo. Sheba is a definite deal breaker." She got to her feet, her fingers trailing along his chest, soaking up the feel of him. "I'm getting champagne, okay? We're having a toast, but it's going to be with the Moet I never opened last night instead of the tequila."

"That tequila is never getting opened," he informed her, capturing her arm and pressing a kiss to the inside of her wrist as he stood. He strode over to the stereo system to turn on some holiday tunes. The Rat Pack crooned about a white Christmas while she tore the foil on the celebratory bottle, excitement already fizzing in her veins.

"We can get back to our game." She found the glasses while he joined her in the kitchen. "Remember? We can take turns deciding what happens after the champagne toast under the Christmas tree?"

Dylan took the bottle from her, easing the cork free with a pop. His eyes held hers with the promise of pleasure as he poured two flutes full of golden bubbles.

"I'll tell you what happens." He put a glass in her hand and, taking his drink, he drew her back out to the living room near the tree decorated in red and gold. "We toast to starting over."

The glow of the Christmas lights refracted off the cut crystal glasses, making the room glisten like a holiday wonderland. She couldn't have staged it better if she'd planned the whole thing out. But then she was fast finding that real life was better than any show.

Dylan lifted his glass and smoothed her hair away from her face. "You first."

Smiling, she considered what she wanted most for Christmas.

"We toast to living happily ever after."

"Then we show each other how much we love each other." His voice softened as he brushed his lips over hers.

"Then we say how much we love each other," she added, feeling dizzy even before she had a sip of her drink.

She kissed him, the moment so perfect she couldn't possibly come up with a better ending.

* * * * *

KAREN FOLEY

IF ONLY IN MY DREAMS

For John, who makes all my dreams come true.

1

SNOWFLAKES FELL SOFTLY against his face, landing on his skin and melting into cool rivulets of water that trickled down his jaw. From somewhere came the sound of church bells, and he remembered that it was almost Christmas. He must be home, with his parents and his siblings, and the knowledge filled him with joy.

Then he remembered there was no snow in his hometown of Monterey. And the church bells were becoming louder, more strident. In fact, they no longer sounded like church bells at all, but just an incessant, intolerable pounding between his temples that was turning whatever gray matter he had left to mush. His body ached. Not the good kind of ache that you got from a hard, physical workout, but the bone-deep ache of illness. Every joint hurt. And he was so hot that he felt a little sick to his stomach. More than a little sick, actually.

He was going to puke.

With a groan, Aiden Cross rolled to his side and retched, but there was nothing in his stomach, and he collapsed onto his back, soaked in sweat and breathing hard. Suddenly, a cold, damp cloth was applied to his forehead, and then it stroked blessed relief along his neck and over his bare chest. He forced himself to open his eyes, wincing at the effort.

A woman bent over him, soothing his fevered skin with the cool cloth. She wore a light brown army T-shirt and a pair of camouflage pants. A stethoscope was draped around her neck, the ends dangling just above her breasts. Her short bob was dark and sleek, and she wore it tucked behind her ears—a style he knew well. How many times had he dreamed of pushing her hair back with his own fingers? He closed his eyes, certain that he must still be dreaming, or delirious with fever.

Lily Munroe, an army medic, had haunted his thoughts since he'd first met her at a joint operations center near the international airport in Entebbe, Uganda, more than six months earlier. But he'd never had such a realistic vision. He cracked his eyes open again, expecting to find himself alone, but she was still there.

When she saw him watching her, she leaned away and came back with a cup in her hand. Sliding an arm behind his shoulders, she lifted him with surprising strength and held the rim to his lips. Something cool and delicious slid past his cracked lips and down his parched throat, and he felt the sweet relief in every cell of his body.

"Here," she coaxed, her voice no more than a whisper. "I want you to take these." She uncurled her fingers to reveal several small, white tablets. "Do you think you can swallow them for me?"

Without waiting for his response, she pushed the pills past his lips and then followed with the cup, giving him no choice but to swallow the tablets.

"Good job." She eased him down again and set the cup aside. "How are you feeling?"

"Like crap." His voice came out as a hoarse croak.

She smiled, revealing a deep dimple in one cheek, but she kept her voice soft and low. "Welcome back to the land of the living, Chief Cross. Do you remember how you got here?"

Aiden peered past her at his surroundings. They were in a large army tent. He was lying on a cot, an IV drip in one arm and nothing but a sheet draped over his body. Mosquito netting surrounded him, pulled back at one side. The air was thick with heat and moisture, clinging to him like a heavy, sticky blanket. A nearby fan stirred the netting, but did little to relieve the discomfort. Someone had strung twinkling, colored lights across the ceiling of the tent, and a rope of green-and-red garland hung over the door.

It was December, although you'd never know it, given the steamy conditions. He remembered being in the jungle with his SEAL unit, tracking a vicious warlord responsible for cutting a swathe of violence through the region. He and his team had been in central Africa for nearly nine months, performing recon missions that lasted anywhere from two to four weeks.

On their most recent mission, they'd been traveling for three weeks when Aiden had begun feeling sick. It had started with chills and a headache, and then a fever. He'd pushed on, willing himself to outlast whatever virus had gotten into his system. But when his headache worsened and the joint and muscle aches began, he could no longer hide the fact that he was seriously ill. He had trouble walking. He was in such intense pain, he felt as if someone had taken a baseball bat to his entire body. The last thing he recalled was hiking through the bush, trying to keep up with his team, and then nothing.

"No," he finally managed, frowning. "I don't remember how I got here."

The effort to recall past events made his head throb. As if she understood, Lily laid the cool cloth back over his temples. "It's okay. Just sleep now. You'll feel better soon, I promise."

She made a movement to rise, and, without meaning to, Aiden put a restraining hand on her arm. She stilled, and her dark gaze dropped to where he held her. Despite the oppressive heat, her skin was cool beneath his fingers. He pulled his hand away, but she remained seated beside him.

"What's wrong with me?" he asked. "Malaria?"

"No. Dengue fever."

No wonder he felt like death. Known locally as breakbone fever, there was no vaccine, no preventative medicine for the mosquito-borne virus and no cure once you contracted it. You simply had to survive it. The most common symptoms were fever and excruciating joint pain.

"How long?"

She gave him a crooked smile, and her dimple made a reappearance. Aiden's gut twisted in a way that had nothing to do with his illness. He still couldn't believe she was here. He'd never expected to see her again. Despite his physical misery, something inside him leaped to life.

"If I didn't know you, I'd assume you were asking how long you've been ill." She paused, and gave him a meaningful look. "But I do know you, so I'm sure what you're really asking is how long before you can rejoin your team and return to the bush. Am I right?"

"Both," he conceded.

His eyes were adjusting to the light, and whatever she had given him must have begun to kick in, because he could look at her without squinting and the pounding behind his eyes was receding to a dull throb. But now that he could focus, he could also see the shadows beneath her eyes and the signs of weariness in her body. Guilt stabbed through him, because he knew without being told that he was the cause of her exhaustion.

"Brad and the others brought you in six days ago." She bent her head and studied her hands, and if she hadn't been Lily Munroe, he'd think she was struggling to contain her emotions. But when she looked up, her expression was shuttered. "You were in pretty bad shape. It took your team three days to reach the base."

The "base" she referred to was little more than a jungle camp—a remote outpost containing several dozen elite troops surrounded by razor wire and cameras. He knew exactly where he was, because he and his unit had helped to carve the camp out of the dense jungle nearly a year earlier. The enormity of what his team had accomplished in getting him to this base was staggering. The region was thick with jungle, and nearly inaccessible. Even dirt roads were scarce. That they'd managed to reach the outpost in just three days told him they'd traveled at top speed, without stopping to sleep.

"Where are they now?"

Lily gave him a tolerant look. "Where do you think? They weren't about to leave until they were sure you'd pull through. They're still here on base."

Aiden groaned. He couldn't believe they'd put the mission on hold in order to drag his sorry ass all the way to the field hospital, which consisted of a tent, six cots and Sergeant Lily Munroe.

He recalled the first time he had seen her at the joint operations command in Entebbe. She'd been the only female assigned to the mission, and with her big dark eyes and curvy body, she'd drawn her share of attention from the younger, single soldiers. But she'd been all business, at least at the beginning, focused on ensuring she had the necessary supplies and equipment to set up a mobile medical unit in the middle of the jungle. Despite the fact she wasn't actually a doctor, most of the guys called her Doc. Except Aiden, he could only think of her as Lily—beautiful, delicate, fragrant.

For the eight weeks they were at the joint operations command, he'd fought his growing attraction to her, knowing their paths were unlikely to ever cross again once they left Entebbe. She hadn't been completely immune to him, either. He'd caught her watching him when she thought he wasn't looking. She might pretend to be all business, but if he'd given her any indication of just how interested he really was, she'd have been all over him. He wasn't being conceited, just realistic.

But as much as he wanted to make their relationship personal—very personal—his mission came first. He'd told himself that he was doing them both a favor by keeping his distance. Any relationship they had would be based solely on sex, and when they finally went their separate ways, she'd be hurt. He'd seen it happen before, and he didn't want to hurt Lily Munroe. So he'd deliberately kept his distance.

And then his buddy and fellow SEAL Brad Dixon had decided she was fair game, and any opportunity Aiden might have had to change his mind was obliterated by the other man's charm and determination to win Lily over. Unlike Aiden, his friend had absolutely no problem with meaningless sex and short-term relationships.

Aiden had come across them kissing once, in Entebbe. They'd broken apart when he'd cleared his throat, and Lily had bolted past him, avoiding his eyes. Beyond that one embrace, he hadn't actually seen proof that they were a couple, but Brad had let him know in no uncertain terms that he and Lily were together in every way that mattered. The knowledge had twisted Aiden's insides, and made him want to smash the other man's face in. But for the sake of the team—they were a unit, after all—he'd contained his jealousy and had tried to forget Lily Munroe. But he hadn't been able to stop thinking about her,

And now here she was, soothing his fevered skin and gazing at him as if she gave a damn whether he lived or died.

He struggled to sit up, but she put her hands on his shoulders and gently pushed him back down on the pillows.

"Easy, sailor," she chided softly. "You're not going any-where. At least not today."

"I'm fine," he insisted. He didn't want her to see him this way, weak and defenseless. And no way would he con-fess to her how much his bones still ached. "I need to get back to my team."

Lily gave him a sympathetic look. "I'm sorry, Chief Cross, but you're in no condition to return to duty."

She was right, of course, but Aiden didn't want to admit it. He hated that he was so weak. So helpless. His entire military career was based on his physical abilities and his intelligence. But right now, he felt as weak as a newborn kitten, and it was all he could do to think straight.

"How long before I can rejoin my team?"

Lily shook her head. "It's hard to say. Dengue fever can be extremely debilitating. You're lucky that you had an uncomplicated strain, but it could be weeks before you're your old self again."

Aiden sharpened his focus on her. "What are you say-ing? That I have to stay in this tent until you say I'm fit for duty?"

Lily smiled.

She was pretty by any standard, but when she smiled, she was breathtaking. Aiden went a little weak in a way that had nothing to do with his illness. In fact, he might actually enjoy being confined to a tent, if Lily Munroe was there with him.

"Actually," she said, "you're going home."

For a moment, Aiden was too stunned to speak. When he did find his voice, it came out as no more than a husky rasp. "What?"

"You're being sent home to recuperate." At his appalled expression, she paused. "This doesn't make you happy."

"No."

Lily leaned forward with an encouraging smile. "You'll be home in time for Christmas."

Christmas.

Under normal circumstances, Aiden would have given his left nut to spend Christmas with his family. Since joining the navy, he could count the number of holidays he'd spent with them on one hand. Did he want to go home?

Hell, yeah.

He thought of his parents, Matthew and Susan Cross. When was the last time he'd hugged his mother, or shaken his father's hand? They'd be getting ready to have the entire extended family over to the house for the holidays, and his dad would be creating yet another holiday-themed martini.

His mom would be going all out with the decorations, bringing out her holiday collections, stringing garland and mistletoe and hanging wreaths throughout the house, including the bedrooms. Together with Aiden's sister and his nieces and nephews, she would bake enough Christmas cookies to swap with the entire neighborhood.

His younger sister Remy had gotten married two years ago, and now she and her husband were expecting their first baby in the spring. He would love to see the telltale bump and share in their excitement. And his older brother, Rob, would bring his wife, his four kids and their dog to the house, ensuring there was sufficient chaos and childish anticipation to go around.

Did Aiden *want* to be a part of that?

Absolutely.

But he *needed* to remain in Africa with his unit.

Lily's words reverberated through his head. *You're being sent home.* Like a boy being expelled from school for bad behavior. He'd never been forced to leave his team behind. Even understanding it was for everyone's benefit, it went against every instinct he had. Unfortunately, he lacked the strength to protest. Instead, he turned his head to the side

and stared at a point beyond Lily, trying to contain his con-
flicting emotions.

So he was unprepared when Lily put a cool hand against
his jaw and gently turned his face until he was staring directly into her eyes.

"You won't do your unit any good by staying here." Her
voice was low but firm. "You need to get better, and the
best place to do that is at home. Get better, and then you
can return to your team." She paused. "Do you know how
many soldiers and sailors would love to be going home for
Christmas?"

Aiden pushed down the surge of guilt that swamped him.
She was right. He was a selfish bastard, and he should be
grateful for this opportunity.

But he wouldn't only be leaving his team; he'd be leaving *her*. He hadn't thought he'd ever see her again after
Entebbe, and now here she was. Maybe the fever was to
blame, but the pull of attraction was even stronger than he
remembered. He'd thought of her—dreamed of her—so
often in the past months, seeing her now was almost more
than he could comprehend.

Before he could respond, the flap of the tent was pushed
open and two men stepped through. Aiden recognized the
first man as his buddy Brad Dixon. Lily stood up abruptly
and stepped away from the bed. Brad's gaze flicked only
briefly to her, but as he walked toward the cot, Aiden didn't
miss how he brushed against Lily, covertly stroking a single finger along the bare skin of her arm. Her eyes flew to
Aiden's, and he knew that she knew he hadn't missed that
small contact.

"Hey, man, how're you feeling?" Brad asked.

Aiden didn't want to talk to Brad. He wanted to drag
him outside and kick his ass. Instead, he reached out and
clasped the other man's hand. "Doing better, thanks to you."

"You're looking better. You were in pretty rough shape."

Aiden glanced at Lily, who was slowly wringing out the washcloth in a basin of water. "Yeah," he said. "That's what Sergeant Munroe said."

"Hey, I'd carry your sorry ass through the jungle anytime." Brad grinned. "You'd do the same for me."

For a brief instant, Aiden privately disagreed with him. "Yeah, I would."

The second man came to stand beside Lily, wearing the same jungle camouflage that she did, and Aiden saw a stethoscope dangling out of the side pocket of his fatigues.

"How's our patient this morning?" he asked, crossing his arms and staring at Aiden as if he were some interesting specimen that he'd found under a rock.

Lily reached for a folder on a side table, opening it to show the doctor the contents. "He's much better. Still running a fever, but at least the convulsions have stopped, and he's lucid. He's no longer dehydrated, and I just gave him something for the pain."

The other man scanned the folder and then closed it and handed it back to Lily. "Excellent." Bending over Aiden, he withdrew a pen light and flashed it into his eyes. "I'm Captain Morse, the new field surgeon. How are you feeling? Are you nauseous?"

Aiden pushed the light away. "I'm fine," he said through gritted teeth. "Never better."

Brad snorted.

Lily touched Brad's sleeve. "Why don't you wait outside until after the doctor examines him? I'll let you know when you can visit."

"Sure." He fist-bumped Aiden. "Glad you're feeling better, bro."

"Yeah." He watched as Lily walked with Brad to the entrance, and they exchanged words that were too low for him to hear. But when Lily came back, her mouth was a thin line, and her expression was shuttered.

After checking his vitals, Captain Morse straightened and scratched some notes on Aiden's medical record.

"You're making good progress." He turned to Lily. "Let's give him a few more days to get some strength back. Meanwhile, I'll contact joint ops and arrange for you both to leave on Friday."

Aiden pushed himself up onto one elbow. "Wait. What do you mean, *both?*"

The field surgeon gave him a surprised look. "You're in no condition to travel alone. Sergeant Munroe's tour is ending, and now that I'm here, we can afford to release her. So we're sending her home with you."

"Well, not to your actual home," Lily said in a rush. "But I'll travel with you as far as Atlanta and make sure you're all set to go home."

Aiden barely suppressed a groan. He was returning to the United States with the one woman he shouldn't be trusted to be alone with, even in his present condition. She was too tempting.

Though the one thing guaranteed to make him keep his distance was the knowledge that she was in a relationship with Brad Dixon. His team member. His SEAL brother. The man who had saved his life.

2

LILY QUIETLY CLOSED her book and glanced over at Aiden. He was asleep beside her, his head against the headrest and his M16 rifle cradled loosely in the crook of his arm. How he could sleep was beyond her, given that they were packed into the military cargo jet like sardines in a tin can. Like all of the hundred or so soldiers on the aircraft, they both wore their combat uniforms. Their helmets and rucksacks were tucked on the floor by their feet, cramping the tight space even more.

They'd been traveling for nearly forty-eight hours, first from the Sudan to an air base in Germany, and now to Fort Benning in Georgia. Once on the ground, they would turn in their weapons and equipment, endure a cursory medical exam and out-briefing and then head to the airport in Atlanta to catch a commercial flight to their final destination.

By the time they'd boarded the enormous aircraft in Germany, Aiden had almost literally been on his last legs. Although he never complained, Lily knew his joints still ached, and she'd forced several pain killers on him. The result was that he'd fallen into a restless sleep. But as uncomfortable as the aircraft was, Lily almost didn't want the flight to end. Once they completed their out-processing at Fort Benning, Aiden would catch a flight to Monterey, and Lily would travel on to Crescent City, California. She doubted their paths would cross again. But for the next few hours, at least, he was hers.

She took the opportunity to study him. Shadows still lingered beneath his eyes, and lines of strain were etched beside his mouth. Despite this, he was hands down the most gorgeous guy she'd ever met. A twinge of guilt pricked her conscience. He wasn't completely well, and yet she couldn't stop thinking about him. Of what it would be like to explore his magnificent body. Of stroking his skin, and feeling him respond to her touch.

No doubt about it—she was a horrible person.

When she'd first seen him at the joint operations command in Entebbe, she'd been unable to stop staring at him. She knew he was a navy SEAL, but he looked more like a surfer—or a movie star—with his tanned skin, sun-streaked hair and startling blue eyes. And when he smiled, her insides turned to liquid. But despite his golden good looks, there was something dangerous about him, and thoroughly masculine. Nobody would ever make the mistake of calling Aiden Cross a pretty boy.

And whenever his eyes were on her, she became uncomfortably aware of herself inside her own skin. If he was near, it took all her effort to focus on her job, and not him.

As the only female on this last mission, she'd become accustomed to a certain amount of masculine attention. But as far as she could tell, Aiden Cross had absolutely no interest in her. She might have been one of the guys for all the notice he took of her as a woman. Several times, when their gazes had met, she'd stared openly at him, letting him see her undisguised interest. But he'd turned away.

So when his friend and fellow SEAL Brad Dixon had come on to her, she hadn't objected, hoping it might rouse some kind of response from Aiden. But again, he'd been coolly disinterested, and Lily had found herself in the awkward position of trying to avoid Brad's advances afterward. She'd been such an idiot, playing adolescent games when she should have been focusing on her job.

That had been easier to do once the SEAL team had left Entebbe, and Aiden Cross was no longer a distraction. But his absence hadn't stopped her from thinking about him, hoping he would return safely. Then on the day his team had arrived at the outpost, pulling his limp body on a makeshift stretcher, she'd thought her worst fears had been realized. She'd actually been relieved to discover he had dengue fever. He would survive.

Aiden stirred restlessly beside her, and she watched his face twitch in sleep. His brow furrowed, and she wanted to lean over and smooth the frown away, as she had done so many times during his illness. In sleep, he was still good-looking, but the full force of his appeal wasn't evident until he opened his eyes. He did so then, groaning a little as he straightened in his seat. Then he turned his gaze to her, and Lily watched, fascinated, as grogginess slowly gave way to awareness.

He pushed himself higher and glanced around at his surroundings. "How long did I sleep?"

"Not long. We'll be landing at Fort Benning soon."

No sooner were the words out of her mouth, than the aircraft gave a violent lurch, and then shuddered through a series of terrifying bumps. A collective mutter of surprise went up from the other soldiers, and without realizing she'd even moved, Lily found herself clutching Aiden's forearm, her fingers digging into the strong muscles.

"Just a little turbulence," Aiden said, surprising her by covering her hand with his.

Lily pulled her hand back. "Sorry. I just wasn't expecting that."

Within seconds, the pilot's voice could be heard over the aircraft's intercom.

"Folks, we're encountering some turbulence as a result of a severe storm moving through the southeastern region. Our controllers on the ground are telling us that conditions at Fort Benning have deteriorated, with a risk of tornadoes in the area. We're diverting to Fort Atterbury in Indiana, instead. We should have you on the ground in ninety minutes."

Lily frowned. "Why Indiana?"

"There are only two military bases set up for out-processing this many returning troops—Fort Benning and Fort Atterbury," Aiden replied.

"But how will this impact our flights to California? Our paperwork says we're leaving from Atlanta," Lily said, beginning to feel the first frissons of alarm finger their way along her spine.

"We'll likely be delayed while they redo our orders."

"You've done this before," Lily guessed.

"A couple of times," he confirmed with a wry smile.

"So how long will it take them to redo our orders and get us out-processed?"

Aiden gave her a sympathetic look. "Let's just say that I wouldn't plan on getting home tonight."

Christmas was just two days away. For herself, she didn't really care where she spent the holiday, even if it was at a military base in the middle of Indiana, but she sensed how much Aiden was anticipating being with his family.

"Maybe they'll get us processed quickly, and we can catch a flight out of Indianapolis in the morning," he said, misinterpreting her expression. "Let me see what I can find out." Reaching into one of his pockets, he withdrew a smartphone and began scrolling through the applications. "There are a couple of flights tomorrow, and the weather looks okay, so as long as we can get through the out-processing reasonably quickly we should be able to get home for Christmas."

Leaning close, he angled the phone so that Lily could see the small screen. She was acutely aware of his nearness and of the way he smelled—like delicious, unadulterated male. Forcing herself to focus on the phone, she read there were indeed several flights leaving Indianapolis the following day.

"Let's just hope they have some seats available," she commented, "or you might end up spending your holiday at Fort Atterbury with me."

She raised her gaze and found herself ensnared in the blueness of Aiden's eyes. Her breath caught at the expression of raw, masculine heat she saw there. He glanced away in the next instant, and Lily wondered if she had only imagined the heat. Then he shoved the phone back in his pocket and crossed his arms, tension radiating from him.

She let out a shaky breath, her heart thudding hard. She hadn't been mistaken. That look had been the one she'd dreamed of seeing on his face, but until this moment, she'd been certain he had no personal interest in her. So what did that look mean? And did she have the courage to do anything about it?

He shifted his gaze back to her and loosened his arms. "Assuming that we *are* able to get a flight out in the morning, are you excited about the holidays?"

Lily thought about going home for the holiday and shrugged. "Christmas has never been a big deal in my family."

She felt Aiden's interest sharpen. "Why not? Is it a religious thing?"

"No." Lily paused and drew in a deep breath. Twenty years had passed since her mother had died, but the story never got easier to tell. "My mom was sick for most of my childhood. She passed away on Christmas Eve, when I was eight. So for my dad, there's been no joy in the Christmas season, only the reminder of what he lost."

"I'm sorry."

Lily nodded. "It's okay."

"No, it's not." Reaching out, Aiden covered her hand with his. "I can't imagine what that must have been like for your family. Do you have brothers and sisters?"

"No. It's just me."

"Please tell me your father at least *tried* to make Christmas special for you."

Lily couldn't look at him. "You have to understand how much my parents loved each other. After my mother was gone, my dad became very depressed. He had no interest in anything, including me."

Aiden made a sound of disgust. "My parents were childhood sweethearts, and they're *still* crazy about each other, but I'm certain that if anything happened to one of them, they'd be there for their kids in every way that mattered."

"I think he just couldn't get out from under the weight of his own grief."

After watching her father suffer, Lily didn't ever want to depend on another person for her happiness, the way her father had depended on her mother. Because if that person left her—or died—she didn't want to experience the kind of pain her father had endured. So while she'd had several relationships since she'd been in the army, none of them had been all that serious, which was how she preferred it.

"I shouldn't pry, but…what was Christmas like for you after your mother passed away?"

Lily thought back to those days. "Well, when I was a teenager, I tried to make Christmas something special. I decorated the house, my friends helped me put up a tree and I even cooked my dad's favorite meal for Christmas dinner…but it didn't make any difference. He didn't care about decorations or presents under the tree or family and friends who wanted to help. He just shut himself away in his bedroom and wouldn't come out until the holidays were over."

As a little girl, Lily had dreamed of a Christmas like the ones her friends had, filled with anticipation of what Santa might bring, of baking cookies and singing carols, of going to a candlelight church service on Christmas Eve. Even when her mother had been alive, she'd been too sick to give more than a nominal effort to celebrating Christmas. There had been a couple of years after her mom's death when Lily's grandparents had brought her to spend Christmas with them. She'd had a glimpse of what Christmas could be like then.

"That's rough," Aiden said, pulling her back to the present. "Maybe you should come spend Christmas with my family."

Lily smiled uncertainly, even as her heart gave a little leap of joy, but in the next instant she decided he was just kidding. "Oh, yeah? Why is that?"

Aiden shrugged, but one corner of his mouth lifted in a smile that could only be called indulgent. "My family tends to go overboard for the holidays. Picture Clark Griswold meets the guy from *Elf*."

Lily raised an eyebrow. "They like to decorate?"

"That's putting it mildly," he said ruefully. "I think my dad's ambition is to put enough lights on the house for it to be visible from outer space."

"Do you have a big family?"

"I have an older brother with four kids, and a younger sister. She's expecting her first baby in the spring. But they'll both be at my parents' house, with their spouses and kids."

"Wow. That sounds fun."

"I don't know that I'd call it fun," he protested, but his mouth curved in a smile. "Chaotic is more like it."

Lily was silent. There had been a time when she would

have given anything to have a brother or sister. But as she'd gotten older, she'd been grateful that she didn't have a sibling to suffer the same loss and disappointment that had marked her own childhood.

She'd enlisted in the army right out of high school, and they had paid for her education and trained her to be a combat medic. In the ten years since, she'd only returned home a handful of times, and those had been strained. Did she want to go home for Christmas? She couldn't think of anything more dismal.

She forced herself to smile, envisioning Aiden at home, surrounded by his family—who would no doubt be ecstatic to have him back for the holidays.

While he hadn't expressed any outward emotion at the prospect of going home, he had been determined to buy Christmas gifts for his parents and siblings, first at the airport in Entebbe, and then at the military base in Germany. He'd chosen his gifts carefully: beautiful scarves and hand-crafted items from Uganda, traditional wooden ornaments and tins of frosted cookies from Germany, along with bottles of mulled wine called glühwein.

Lily had purchased a Bavarian-style hat and a box of fine cigars for her father, although she couldn't imagine he'd have a use for either. As far as she could tell, he spent all his time tinkering in his garage, repairing small engines and appliances and then reselling them. He rarely went anywhere, except to the local diner, where he ate nearly all his meals.

"Chaotic," she repeated now, aware her voice sounded a little wistful. "That actually sounds perfect."

She sensed Aiden watching her, but before he could respond, the aircraft pitched sharply, and Lily found herself thrown against Aiden's shoulder. He steadied her, but even after the aircraft resumed a smooth path, he kept one hand wrapped warmly around her hers. This time, Lily didn't pull away.

"Yeah," he replied, "my family does a good job of making the holidays memorable."

"You said your parents were childhood sweethearts," she said, staring down at their linked hands. "And they're still married. That's really nice to hear."

"Yeah, it's one of the reasons why I—" He broke off abruptly, looking embarrassed. "Never mind."

"No, tell me what you were going to say," Lily insisted, smiling. She found his sudden discomfiture oddly appealing.

"Nah, it's…personal," he muttered, clearly uncomfortable.

Lily laughed. "Now I have to know—tell me."

He gazed at her, and something in his expression caused her heart to stutter in her chest.

"I was going to say that my parents are my role models." He lowered his voice so that only Lily could hear him. "A lot of the guys I know—guys in my unit—don't mind casual relationships. They don't want anything long-term. In fact, for some of them, all they want is a quick hookup."

Lily averted her gaze and chewed her lip. Was he referring to Brad Dixon? Brad had made it clear that he was interested in sleeping with Lily, but he'd never really tried to get to know her. Not that Lily had wanted him to—she had absolutely no interest in Brad.

"So what are you saying?" she asked carefully.

He bent his head until he was looking directly into her eyes. "I'm not one of those guys. I don't do one-night stands, or casual relationships."

There was no denying the sincerity in his voice, and the knowledge should have made Lily happy. Instead, a sense of discouragement washed over her. Casual relationships— like the ones she had.

She forced herself to smile, and injected what she hoped was mild amusement into her voice. "So you're saying you only ever get involved with women you think you might eventually marry?" She made a soft scoffing noise. "That's pretty limiting, isn't it? Not to mention idealistic."

He leaned toward her, and his voice dropped to no more than a whisper. "I'm just saying that when I get involved with a woman, it means something beyond just great sex. I want a commitment."

His breath was warm against her temple, and Lily felt a shiver go through her, because she knew that sex with Aiden Cross *would* be great. How many times had she imagined what it would be like to be with him?

"A commitment?" she asked lightly. "Why? I mean, what would be the point? Take it from someone who knows—nothing lasts forever. You're better off settling for the great sex."

She sensed Aiden's surprise, followed by his withdrawal, and immediately regretted her words. She told herself again that she wouldn't get serious about any man, no matter how appealing he might be. She'd experienced firsthand what happened when you loved someone and then lost that person. She didn't ever want to go through that again.

3

THE PROCESSING CENTER at Fort Atterbury was packed with soldiers. They either stood in line to return their equipment, or sprawled in chairs or on the floor as they waited. Aiden and Lily had stood in line for nearly three hours just to turn in their weapons. Then, along with the other soldiers on their flight, they'd been directed to an enormous hangar to wait for their medical exams. The hangar was filled with yet more soldiers, who watched television or texted their loved ones as they waited. The scene was a little surreal, as the hangar's interior was festive with holiday decorations in direct contrast to the palpable frustration of the troops.

Aiden's joints ached, and he felt a little sick from lack of sleep, but there was no way he'd let Lily know. She'd already done so much for him, and he didn't want her to continue thinking of him as her patient. He was improving every day; he just needed to get a good night's sleep. They were both carrying their duffel bags and their military-issued backpacks, stuffed with their Christmas purchases. Finding a spot against the wall, they set their gear down and surveyed the scene. They also each carried a stack of forms that had to be completed before they could proceed to the mandatory checkpoints.

A display screen at the front of the hangar periodically

flashed numbers, and Aiden glanced at his paperwork. The number he'd been assigned was literally hundreds away from the number currently being served.

Lily turned to Aiden and gave him a swiftly assessing look that had nothing to do with feminine interest and everything to do with her medical training. "You need rest."

Aiden bristled. "I'm fine," he said tightly. He didn't want Lily viewing him as weak, or as someone who needed to be coddled. "At this rate, we won't be going anywhere for hours."

Lily's shoulders sagged. She was tired, too, although she'd never admit it. "So what are our options?"

Aiden glanced around, weighing their choices. "I'm not sure we have any. I'll get a read on how long before our numbers are called."

Before he could do so, however, an enlisted soldier walked to the front of a tent with a microphone.

"Listen up," he directed. "The MEDDAC is now closed. You'll be directed to another hangar where you'll spend the night. MEDDAC will reopen in the morning at 0600 hours. If you do not get through your medical in-processing by 1600 hours tomorrow, you'll have to spend Christmas here at Fort Atterbury."

Lily turned to Aiden in astonishment. "That can't be right. Why is it taking them so long to in-process everyone?"

"The storms likely diverted hundreds of troops from Fort Benning to Fort Atterbury, and they're probably shorthanded. Not all the staff are military, and civilians may have already checked out for the holidays."

Rising, they hefted their duffel bags over their shoulders and followed the throng of soldiers out of the hangar and along a road. The temperature had plummeted to below freezing, and the ground was slick with a coating of ice.

"Watch your step," Aiden advised, and would have put

a hand beneath Lily's elbow, but knew she wouldn't thank him for it.

They reached a series of hangars and paused at the entrance to the first one, where the male troops were spending the night. The entire interior was lined with rows of metal bunk beds, but all the beds had already been claimed. The new soldiers, unable to find a vacant cot, simply threw their gear on the floor and tried to make themselves comfortable.

"You can't spend the night here," Lily said with dismay. "They don't even have enough beds for everyone."

"It's fine," he muttered. "I've slept in worse places."

Lily turned to him, and Aiden recognized the stubborn set of her jaw. "You're not staying here tonight, Aiden."

He thought for a moment, and then realized there was no reason why they should have to stay, as long as they returned in the morning for their medical exams.

"Okay, fine," he agreed. "Let's see if we can get a taxi and find a hotel for the night on our own."

They went back to the main hangar, where hundreds of soldiers were still milling around, apparently having decided that sleeping in a chair was preferable to sleeping on the floor in the bunk house. For himself, he wouldn't have minded, but Lily needed rest. After what she'd told him, he wanted something better for her than another ruined Christmas. As he watched, two civilian women walked toward the exit, pulling on their coats. Aiden moved quickly to intercept them.

"Excuse me," he said, giving them his most charming smile, "but can you tell me if there are any hotels around the base? I don't mind paying for a room, I just want to find a place where we can get some rest."

The first woman took in his uniform, and then glanced beyond him to where Lily stood guard over their duffel bags.

"Every hotel in the area is filled to capacity," she said.

"We don't typically receive this many returning troops and we don't have room for everyone, so we sent the officers and the senior enlisted to the nearby hotels."

Aiden glanced at Lily, noting how her slender shoulders bowed beneath the weight of her backpack, and he found he could barely contain his growing impatience. "So what does that mean? That we're stuck here in the hangar until we can get our out-processing completed?"

The two women looked at each other, and the first seemed to come to a decision. "If you want to come with me, I'll see if I can find something for you. I have a friend who operates a bed-and-breakfast on the river. I'm not sure if she has any vacancies, but at least it's a place to stay."

Aiden nodded. "I don't care about the cost. We've been traveling for more than two days and just need a place to crash until we can get out of here."

"That might not be anytime soon," the woman cautioned. "You're virtually last on the list, with a whole lot of soldiers in front of you and the flights are already pretty booked."

"Yeah, I got that. Anything you can do to get us out of this hangar is appreciated."

He and Lily followed the two women to a vacant desk tucked behind a partition and waited while one of them made a phone call.

"My friend says she has only one room available, and it's small," she finally said, covering the phone.

"Fine." Aiden nodded. "We'll take it."

"Aiden—" Lily stared at him.

"We can ask for a cot," he said, reading the expression on her face. "And if there's no cot, there's always the floor. Don't worry so much."

She looked indignant. "The only thing I'm worried about is your health."

Aiden shot her a tolerant gaze. "Don't. I'm fine."

He listened as the woman made the final arrangements, and then hung up the phone.

"The bed-and-breakfast is about five miles from here. I go right past it on my way home, so if you'd like, I can give you a ride. You'll just have to take a taxi in the morning," she said. She quickly scribbled a number on a piece of paper. "But call me first. This number will connect you directly to my desk, and I can tell you how long the wait will be."

"Great." Aiden tucked the paper into his breast pocket. "Thank you."

Hefting his duffel bag over his shoulder, he took Lily's arm as they followed the woman toward the exit. Outside, the wind was so frigid it snatched his breath away. He bent his head into the force of it as he drew Lily into the shelter of his shoulder and led her toward a parking lot where the woman's car was parked. Opening the back door, he pushed Lily inside, taking her duffel bag and putting it in the trunk with his own. Climbing in beside her, he leaned forward.

"Thanks again," he said to the woman. "You don't know what this means to both of us."

The woman smiled as she started the engine. "It's my pleasure. My name is Ann Norton, by the way. I'll have you both at Gingerbread Cottage in no time. The owner, Inge, is a good friend of mine. I know you'll be comfortable there tonight."

"Gingerbread Cottage?" Lily finally asked, as they drove away from the base, her expression a mixture of disbelief and laughter. "Are you kidding?"

"I'm not," Ann replied. "The cottage is a little bit of a misnomer, since it's actually a large house, but I think you'll love it."

Lily angled her head to glance at Aiden, amusement dancing in her eyes. He shrugged, but an answering smile pulled at his mouth. "You can't make this stuff up."

The drive to the bed-and-breakfast was painstakingly slow. There were almost no other cars on the roads, which were slippery with ice.

"A little different than the African jungle," Lily mused. "I didn't think I'd ever miss the heat."

"You sure complained enough about it," Aiden teased. She stared at him in surprise. "Did I?"

"Yes." He laughed. "You said you hated being hot and sticky. So...do you?"

"Do I what?"

"Miss the heat?"

Lily stared at him for a long moment, as if trying to decipher some hidden meaning in his words.

"Yes," she finally said, her voice soft. "Actually, I do miss it."

Aiden knew he shouldn't ask—hell, he shouldn't even *care*—but he couldn't stop the words from spilling out of his mouth.

"And Brad? Do you miss him, too?"

For a moment she looked at him as if she had no idea what he was talking about. "Who?"

"Brad Dixon. Your boyfriend."

He watched the expressions that chased themselves across her face—surprise, guilt and then a sort of resignation.

"Brad isn't my boyfriend," she finally said. "Where did you even get that idea?"

"From Brad." Aiden hated that his emotions were still so strong when he thought about Lily with Brad.

She closed her eyes briefly, and then looked directly at him. "I might have given Brad the wrong idea back in Entebbe," she said in a low voice. "But there was never anything serious between us. I don't do serious."

"I saw you," he pressed. "With Brad, kissing him."

"No," she protested, her voice surprisingly forceful.

"You saw Brad kissing *me*. I was *not* kissing him back, and if that's what you thought, then—then you thought wrong."

More than anything, he wanted to be wrong, but Brad had said that he and Lily had *a thing*. Aiden's sense of honor would keep him from so much as touching Lily if he thought she was committed to another man. But he believed her when she said there was nothing between her and Brad. And in retrospect, he wondered if Brad's words had been more boasting than anything else. Which meant he was about to spend the night with the single Lily Munroe.

"Here we are," Ann said, interrupting his thoughts. "If I know Inge, she'll have a fire going inside, so you should have your heat in no time."

Aiden exchanged a glance with Lily, and then bent forward to look through the window at the bed-and-breakfast. Lights were on inside the pretty Victorian house, lending it a warm, welcoming glow. Aiden could see why it was called the Gingerbread Cottage. The roofline and windows were trimmed in decorative scrollwork, so that the house resembled something from a child's storybook. Candles glowed in each window, and outside, beside the door, an evergreen tree twinkled with bright lights beneath a glittering layer of ice.

"Oh," Lily breathed in awe, as she leaned over his shoulder for a better look. "It's like a fairy-tale house."

"More like a doll's house," Aiden grunted, but her obvious pleasure made him equally pleased that they would spend the night there. Maybe he could rescue this Christmas for her, after all.

Thanking Ann again, and promising he would call in the morning before they returned to the base, he indicated that Lily should go ahead while he retrieved their duffel bags from the trunk.

"I can get my own bag," she insisted, shivering in the frigid cold.

Aiden wanted to argue with her, but more than that, he wanted her inside and out of the weather, so he just nodded and handed the heavy bag to her. Besides, as he hefted his own bag over his shoulder, he realized he was running out of steam. Every joint in his body ached, and a dull throb had begun to drum behind his eyes. Bending his head against the icy wind, he followed Lily along the walk to the front door, which was opened before they even had a chance to knock.

A middle-aged woman stood aside to let them in, and Aiden followed Lily into a tall foyer that was strung with evergreen garlands and mistletoe. The woman was small and round, with her brown hair worn in a braid wrapped around her head. A red-and-white striped apron protected her clothes, and Aiden detected a smudge of flour on one cheek. As he stepped inside, he closed his eyes and breathed deeply, inhaling the warm, fragrant scent of cinnamon and ginger, and his mouth watered. From somewhere deep in the house, he could hear the strains of Christmas music.

"Come in, come in," the woman exclaimed, waving goodbye to Ann before she closed the heavy door behind them, firmly shutting out the wild weather. "I'm Inge Buchwald. Welcome to Gingerbread Cottage." She surveyed their uniforms and duffel bags. "Well, you must be exhausted. Let me show you to your room, and you can relax for a bit. Then, if you're interested, you can join us for a refreshment. I just made a fresh batch of cookies."

She turned toward a wide staircase, whose decorative balustrade was wound with garland. Glancing at Lily, who was staring after the woman with something like awe, he followed Inge up the curving stairs.

"It's fortunate that I have a room available," Inge was saying over her shoulder. "I normally close the cottage for the holiday, since my family comes to stay. But the storms in the south prevented my older daughter and her husband from joining us, so I have just one room available."

They reached the top of the staircase, and Aiden saw they were in a long corridor with a deep, cushioned window seat at the end and another staircase that wound its way to the third floor of the enormous Victorian.

"Here we are," Inge said, pausing at a door near the end of the hallway. "This is my favorite room. It's small, but I think you'll be quite comfortable here."

Aiden stepped inside and dropped his duffel bag and backpack onto the floor. Lily came to stand beside him with a softly indrawn breath. He didn't dare look at her. An enormous canopy bed with a white crocheted bedspread and a delicate lace canopy dominated the room. Two red-and-white striped peppermint candies rested on the lacy pillows. A small fire burned in a fireplace at the foot of the bed, and two cozy, upholstered chairs had been drawn up close to its warmth. A Christmas wreath hung over the mantel, and the deep window seats had been strung with tiny, twinkling lights.

"There's a small bathroom through that door," Inge said. "You'll find everything you need. My family and I will be in the parlor for several hours yet, so please come down and join us for some hot chocolate and cookies. There's usually a board game or a card game going on if you're interested. But if you're tired, I can send up a pot of tea or cocoa for you to enjoy in the room."

Aiden glanced at his watch. It was barely nine o'clock, but his entire body ached for sleep. The last thing he wanted was to go downstairs and be sociable.

"Thank you," Lily said, before he could respond. "But we've been traveling for two days, and I'm not sure I can keep my eyes open for another minute. If you don't mind, I think we'll just call it a night."

"I understand," Inge said, her voice sympathetic. "You

look exhausted. Sleep as late as you'd like, and come down when you're ready. We usually serve breakfast between seven and ten o'clock, but if you need to be up earlier, just help yourself to anything in the kitchen."

After she left, an awkward silence settled over the room. Aiden cleared his throat. "I'll take the floor."

"Don't be ridiculous. You're still recovering, and you need your rest. I'll take the floor."

Aiden gave her a tolerant look. "You're not sleeping on the floor." He frowned. "In fact, I'm not sure there's enough room for *anyone* to sleep on the floor."

The room was comfortable enough, with its sitting area in front of the fireplace and the large canopy bed, but they'd have to push the chairs aside in order to clear some floor space.

Lily drew in a deep breath. "Even if one us was willing to sleep on the floor, there really isn't a need. We're both adults. The bed is enormous. I think we can agree to share, if we just lay some ground rules."

She was adorable in her earnestness, and he barely suppressed a grin at the way she anxiously twisted her hands.

"Ground rules?" he repeated.

"Sure." She indicated the bed. "You know, like staying on our own side of the bed."

"And that's it?"

She gave him a bright smile. "Yeah."

"Okay, agreed." He gave her what he hoped was a serious nod of agreement.

"Good." She pushed her fingers through her hair. "God, I need a shower."

Aiden watched as she unzipped her duffel bag and rummaged through the contents. He caught a glimpse of something lacy and pink before she wadded the scrap of fabric up inside an army T-shirt. Then, grabbing a small cosmetic bag, she tucked everything under one arm and made her way to the bathroom.

"I won't be long," she called, "and then it's all yours."

Walking over to the bed, Aiden flung himself across the mattress and stared up at the lace canopy.

He was alone in a room with Lily Munroe. She was interested. He was interested. He knew what could happen tonight, if he let it. But he'd been serious when he'd told Lily that he didn't do casual. If he thought she'd consider more than just a one-time hookup, he wouldn't hesitate to let her know exactly how he felt about her. But she'd made it clear that she didn't want a serious relationship. So, as far as he was concerned, they'd reached an impasse.

And yet, as he heard the shower turn on, he couldn't prevent his imagination from picturing Lily, naked and wet beneath the steaming spray. With a groan, he closed his eyes.

It was going to be a long night.

4

LILY SHOWERED QUICKLY, unable to stop thinking about the man in the other room. *The man she was about to share a bed with.* She couldn't believe how quickly things had changed, and recalled again their conversation in the taxi cab. He'd thought she was involved with Brad Dixon. He wasn't completely wrong, and she had only herself to blame for giving him that impression. Remembering how she had led Brad on made her feel ashamed. She'd only done it in order to make Aiden jealous, and it had completely back-fired on her.

But now Aiden knew the truth…except for the part about why she had encouraged Brad. She wasn't sure she'd ever have the courage to tell him why she'd done that. She brushed her teeth and then quickly toweled her hair dry, running her fingers through it to loosen the tangles before pulling on the clean panties and the T-shirt along with a pair of loose shorts that she'd brought in with her. There was nothing about her clothing that was immodest, but her heart pounded with anticipation as she prepared to go back into the bedroom.

She opened the bathroom door, immediately finding Aiden sprawled across the bed. As Lily cautiously approached, she realized he had fallen asleep. Creeping closer, she bent over him, fascinated, even though she'd seen every inch of his body when she'd cared for him during his illness. He'd removed his camouflage jacket and wore a light brown T-shirt that stretched across the taut muscles of his chest and shoulders. Although he'd lost some weight as a result of the fever, he was still supremely fit and uncompromisingly male.

His face was turned to the side, and his lashes lay dark against his chiseled cheekbones. A light stubble of golden whiskers covered his jaw and throat, and Lily's fingertips itched with the urge to rub over the bristled skin. One of his hands rested on his flat stomach, and she watched the even rise and fall of his chest. He looked so peaceful and she didn't want to wake him up. Quietly, she shook out the extra blanket that lay folded neatly on the foot of the bed and leaned over to cover him with it.

At the first touch of the blanket, however, he came violently awake, grabbing her by the upper arms as he surged to a sitting position, his eyes searching wildly around the room for any perceived danger, before returning to her face. Too startled by his reaction to speak, Lily could only stare back at him.

"I was dreaming," he said, his voice rough with sleep. Slowly, he released her arms, but slid one hand to the nape of her neck, preventing her from pulling away. "Of you."

Lily stopped breathing. He was so close that she felt the warmth of his breath against her cheek, saw the varying striations of color in the incredible blueness of his eyes. When he drew her down, she didn't resist, but welcomed the press of his mouth against hers. His lips were warm and firm, and with a soft sigh, she leaned into him.

He gathered her closer, one hand sliding around her waist to settle at the small of her back, while he cradled her cheek in his other hand and deepened the kiss. Lily was only vaguely aware of putting one hand on his shoulder for balance before he rolled over and pulled her beneath him on the bed. The change in their positions allowed Lily to wind her arms around his neck as he braced himself over her, kissing her with a sensuousness that made her bare toes curl.

A sudden knock on the door interrupted them, and Aiden pulled away, looking a little dazed. Lily sat up and dragged in a deep breath, feeling flushed and breathless.

"I'll get it," she offered, springing up to open the door. A young woman stood there with a tray in her hands. A boy of about six or seven peeked out from behind her.

"Hi," the woman said with a smile, glancing past Lily and into the room. "I hope I'm not disturbing you. I'm Inge's daughter, Abby. This is my son, Josh." She held out the tray. "We thought you might like some hot tea or cocoa, and my mother sent up some of her cookies. They just came out of the oven."

"Thank you." Lily took the tray from her hands. "This looks wonderful."

"Great. Well, have a good night."

Lily closed the door with her hip and carried the tray over to a small table near the fireplace. On the tray was a teapot filled with steaming water, two matching teacups next to a plate of gingerbread cookies and a canister of whipped cream. A small basket contained tea bags and envelopes of powdered hot chocolate. The basket was adorned by two candy canes, tied together with a slender red ribbon. Still shaken by the intensity of Aiden's kiss, she concentrated on the tray, unable to meet his eyes.

"I hope you're hungry," she said lightly. "There's enough hot chocolate and cookies here to feed a small army."

Aiden pushed himself off the bed and scrubbed his hands over his face. "Lily, about what just happened—"

"Forget it," she said, and gave him a quick smile. "I know what it's like to wake up and have no idea where you

are or what's going on. Like you said—you were dreaming. It's fine."

He frowned. "No, that's not what I meant."

Lily didn't want to hear him say that kissing her had
been a mistake, not when it had felt so *right* to her. He'd
told her that he didn't do casual, and she knew Aiden Cross
was one of those guys who put honor above everything.
But for that one moment, she wanted to believe that he had
kissed her because he wanted to—because he couldn't help
himself. Desperate to stop him from minimizing the kiss,
she snatched a cookie from the plate and held it out to him.

"Here, try this."

He obediently took a bite and gave a soft hum of appre-
ciation. Reaching out, he took the remaining part of the
cookie from her hand.

"Is it good?" she asked unnecessarily. From the expression on his face, he was having an unforgettable experience.

"Here," he answered. "Try it."

Before Lily guessed his intent, he broke off a piece of
the gingerbread cookie and pressed it against her lips. She
accepted it automatically, chewing and letting the exquisite flavor explode in her mouth. Aiden hadn't removed his
hand, and now he brushed his thumb across her lower lip.

"Delicious," Lily agreed, when she could speak.

"Yeah," he murmured, and shifted closer, his gaze on
her mouth. "Delicious."

He was going to kiss her. She raised herself on her toes
to meet him, inwardly rejoicing. She wanted this—wanted
him. She'd craved his touch since the moment she'd first
laid eyes on him nearly nine months ago. Now he covered
her mouth in a kiss that was both soft and firm, tasting her,
and he made the same hum of pleasure deep in his throat
that he'd made when he'd eaten the cookie.

When he finally pulled back, his eyes were bluer than

she'd ever seen them, seeming to glow against his tanned skin. He tipped his forehead against hers.

"Okay, now I definitely need to take a shower," he said in a rueful tone. "A cold one."

Lily nodded, momentarily at a loss for words. She watched as he moved away from her and unzipped his duffel bag to pull out a clean pair of clothes and a toiletry bag, before going into the bathroom and closing the door behind him. Lily sank into the nearest armchair and drew in a shaky breath.

She was trembling all over. Just the memory of that kiss made her feel a little boneless. She sagged back in the chair, feeling elated and nervous all at the same time. She wanted to laugh out loud with delight, and she pressed her fingers against her mouth to prevent herself from making any noise. She heard the shower turn on, and the images that ran through her mind were so explicit that she knew she had to find a distraction.

Glancing at her watch, she saw it was nine-thirty. She'd called her father from the airport in Germany to tell him she would be home that night. He'd sounded both pleased and a little panicky, explaining that he hadn't yet bought a Christmas tree. He didn't say so, but Lily had known that he hadn't bought any gifts, either. She'd assured him that she didn't need a tree, and that spending time with him was all she wanted for Christmas.

A lie.

Because faced with the choice of spending the holiday at home with her father or here with Aiden, she'd choose the latter every time. Feeling like a bad daughter, she pulled her cell phone out of her backpack and quickly dialed her father. She listened as the phone rang on the other end, a little relieved when it went to voice mail. In the bathroom, she heard the water turn off.

"Hi, Dad," she said into the phone. "It's me, Lily. Our

flight got diverted, and now we're grounded due to a huge storm system. I'm not sure I'll be able to get another flight out tomorrow. In fact, it's looking like I might not be able to get home for Christmas, after all. So I hope you didn't go to any trouble and get a tree. I know how much you hate that stuff." She paused. "I'm staying at a bed-and-breakfast near Fort Atterbury, called the Gingerbread Cottage. It's really sweet. Well, I'll call you tomorrow when I have some more news. Bye, Dad."

She hung up the phone, guiltily relieved that she hadn't been able to reach him. She should be happy—she didn't need to hear his false good cheer, telling her how much he was looking forward to her visit, when she knew it wasn't true. She'd been home a half dozen times in the ten years since she'd joined the army, and during those visits, he'd always been a little uncomfortable around her, as if he wasn't sure what to say to her. In fact, she always got the sense she was somehow interfering with his routine, which seemed to revolve around the meals he ate at the local diner. But there was a part of her that was still childish enough to want her father to miss her. Sighing, she turned around just as the bathroom door opened.

And her breath caught.

Aiden stood silhouetted in the doorway, his impressive body wreathed in steam, wearing nothing but a pair of shorts. He stepped into the room, seemingly unaware of how Lily gaped at him. Seeing him naked and unconscious was one thing—seeing him nearly naked, with all his glorious muscles in perfect, mouthwatering, flexible condition was another thing altogether.

"Who were you talking to?" he asked.

"My father," she said, dragging her thoughts away from his physique. "Only, he didn't answer, so I had to leave a message. Hopefully, he isn't at the airport waiting for my flight to arrive." She frowned. "Are you feeling okay? You look flushed."

"Yeah, it's warm in here," he said, dropping his T-shirt onto the bed and shoving his folded uniform back into the duffel bag. "I thought the jungle was hot, but between the shower and the fire, this room is a sauna."

Forgetting her lustful thoughts, Lily moved immediately to his side. Ignoring his startled expression, she placed the back of her hand against his forehead. His skin was warm and still damp from his shower, but she didn't detect any sign of fever. Still not convinced, she put her hand on his wrist, checking his pulse as she watched the seconds tick by on the bedside clock. Was it only her imagination, or did his heart rate seem a little high?

"I'm fine," Aiden said irritably, pulling free from her hold. "Just a little overheated, and dead tired."

"Sorry," Lily murmured, crossing her arms and tucking her hands against her body, lest she be tempted to touch him again. "I guess I can't always turn off the medic in me. But you should probably take some painkillers before you turn in. That way you'll at least get a good night's sleep."

He gave her a lopsided grin, and before she could guess his intent, he reached out and pushed a strand of her damp hair behind her ear. "I don't want any painkillers."

Lily swallowed hard and tried to act as if his touch wasn't having an explosive effect on her heart rate. Or her body temperature. Or her limbs, which felt suddenly very weak. "Why not?"

"They give me really bizarre dreams, and I wake up more tired than if I didn't take anything. Besides, I don't want you treating me like I'm still sick. I'm not."

Lily nodded. "I know. It's just that with dengue fever, the fever can sometimes recur." Correctly interpreting his warning look, she lifted one hand. "But I see that's not the case with you. You're just tired."

"Thank you," he said, with exaggerated emphasis.

"So how long is the navy giving you to rest up?" she asked. While Lily knew he'd been sent home to recuperate, she didn't know how long they would allow him to recover before he had to return to duty.

Aiden shrugged. "Six weeks, and then they'll perform another health assessment. If everything goes well, I should be back with my unit by February. What about you? Do you get a break before you need to report to your next assignment?"

"I would if I had a next assignment." Sensing his attention sharpen, she lifted one shoulder in a shrug. "This is it for me. I'm getting out."

"Why?"

"It's just time. I've been doing the army thing for ten years, and now I'm ready to do something different."

"Like what?"

"Well… I thought I'd go back to school and become a pediatric nurse. Maybe work at a local hospital." She sensed his surprise. "What? You think I'm making a mistake?"

"No, I THINK it's a great plan," Aiden said, and he realized he meant it. He liked thinking Lily would be safe in one place. He liked thinking of her in nursing scrubs, taking care of children. Most of all, he liked to think that if she was willing to put down roots, maybe she'd be willing to consider a committed relationship.

With him.

"What about you?" she asked. "Do you plan on staying with the SEALs?"

"For now, I do." Aiden had a life plan, and it involved a career as a navy SEAL, at least until he had a family of his own. Then he would get out of special ops and become an instructor. He didn't ever want his wife worrying that he might not come home from an assignment. But he wouldn't share any of that with Lily. At least, not yet. They were treading dangerous waters, so he sought safer territory.

"Why don't we have a cup of hot chocolate and turn in? With luck, we'll get through the processing in time to catch a flight before noon tomorrow."

"Sounds good."

LILY TRIED TO FOCUS on pouring two cups of hot chocolate, but her gaze continued to slide toward Aiden and all that smooth, tanned skin, and she ended up sloshing the hot water over her fingers. With a soft exclamation, she set the teapot down and flapped her hand.

"Hey, are you okay?" Aiden came to her side and took her hand in his, inspecting it. "You should run this under cold water."

"It's fine," she said, feeling herself go warm beneath his regard. "The water was hot, but not hot enough to do any damage. It just surprised me more than anything."

"Well, you're the medic, so I'll have to take your word for it." He released her hand, but he was still so close that she could feel the heat that rolled off his body. His gorgeous, muscled chest was right there, blocking out everything else.

Turning away abruptly, she gave each cup of cocoa a brisk stir and picked up the canister of whipped cream, holding it up. "Do you want some?"

"Sure. Load me up."

Lily had a sudden, vivid image of herself covering those delicious pectorals in whipped cream and then licking it from his body. Her hand trembled a bit as she sprayed the cream into the mug and handed it to him, then she picked up her own mug. Lily watched him sip the hot chocolate, fascinated when he used his tongue to lick the whipped cream from his lips. She wanted to do the same thing.

He looked at her over the rim of his mug, and she was certain he must see the naked desire in her eyes. She bent her head and took a hasty gulp of hot chocolate to hide her confusion. They drank in silence for several moments before Aiden set his nearly empty cup down on the tray. Picking up the T-shirt he'd discarded earlier, he pulled it on. Lily tried to conceal her disappointment.

"I'm going to make a few phone calls," he said. "So if you want to change and get ready for bed, I can either go into the bathroom, or step out into the hall."

"Why would you do that?"

"To give you some privacy."

Setting her mug down, Lily spread her arms. "For what? This is it, Chief Cross. I'm as ready for bed as I'm ever going to be, so if you were expecting sexy lingerie, I'm sorry to disappoint you."

He flushed. "Of course I wasn't expecting sexy lingerie." He met her eyes. "And for the record, I'm not disappointed. You look great, no matter what you're wearing."

Now it was Lily's turn to go warm. "I wasn't fishing for compliments."

Aiden threw up his arms, and then gestured toward the door. "I'm going to step out into the hall, and you can do whatever it is you need to do to get ready for bed, okay? I'll make my phone calls, and then I'll come back." He paused. "I realize this isn't an ideal situation, but you're safe with me, Lily. I hope you know that."

She did. Aiden Cross would never do anything to make her nervous or uncomfortable. Sadly, there was a part of her that wished he would. But she nodded and gave him what she hoped was a grateful smile.

"Thanks. I appreciate that."

He paused as if he would say something more, and then seemed to reconsider. He turned and slipped out of the room, and a few minutes later, Lily could hear him speaking in quiet tones. With a sigh, she shut off all the lights in the room except the small table lamp on Aiden's side of the bed. Then, walking around to the far side of the bed, she pulled back the comforter and slid between the sheets.

From where she lay, she could see the wind bending the branches of a tree outside her window. The force of it rattled the window panes, but inside the room, she was warm and snug. The fire had died to glowing embers in the grate, and she could still smell fresh gingerbread. In a few minutes, the sexiest man alive was going to pull back the blankets on the bed, and climb in beside her.

She thought about what he said. *You're safe with me.*

She had no doubt of that. But she wondered how he would react if she told him her one and only Christmas wish was to be in his arms? To have him make love to her?

Sighing, she turned on her side and bunched the pillow beneath her cheek, knowing from experience that not all Christmas wishes came true.

5

AIDEN DREAMED HE was at home, in his old bedroom, and he was scared crapless that his parents might walk in on him because he had a girl in his bed. His folks weren't prudish, but they'd certainly object if they found out he was having sex under their roof. There were some things you just didn't do.

But he was fully aroused, and so horny that he didn't care.

The girl was pressed against him, her breath warm against his neck. In his dream, he couldn't see her face, but it didn't matter. Her skin felt like hot silk beneath his questing hands. She was soft and supple, and she smelled incredible.

He wanted to lick her everywhere.

"Aiden?" Her voice was a whisper.

"Yeah, baby." He pressed against her so that she knew how ready he was. He wanted—*needed*—to be inside her. But she had too many clothes on, so he slid his hand into the back of her pants to cup and squeeze her ass.

"Aiden."

Not so much a whisper this time as a shocked gasp. She squirmed in his arms and pressed her hands against his chest, trying to push him away.

Opening his eyes, he slowly became aware that he wasn't dreaming—*this was real*. Recollection flooded back. He wasn't at his parents' house. He was at a bed-and-breakfast.

The faceless girl of his dreams was, in fact, Lily Munroe. And he had his hand down her shorts, cupping her delectable rear end.

"Jesus, Lily." His voice came out as a husky rasp.

She stopped struggling. "You're awake."

Oh, yeah. And still hard and aching. The uncomfortable reality of the situation should have been enough to cool his rampant lust, but discovering Lily pressed against him was only fueling his growing need. Still, he'd promised that she would be safe with him, so he reluctantly withdrew his hand from her shorts and rolled onto his back.

"Sorry," he muttered. "I was dreaming."

"It's okay," she said, surprising him. He sensed her rise up on one elbow beside him, and as his eyes adjusted to the darkness, he could make out her face. "You were making noises in your sleep," she murmured, "and I thought your joints might be aching."

Aiden gave a huff of laughter. Definitely not his joints. "I'm sorry I woke you. Go back to sleep." She didn't move, just studied him. "What?"

"What were you dreaming about?" Her voice sounded a little breathless.

"Lily," he groaned. "I think it's pretty apparent what I was dreaming about." *Licking her.* "I had my hand down your freaking pants."

To his shock, she laid her free hand on his chest. The heat of her fingers burned through the thin material of his T-shirt. He wondered if she could feel his unsteady heartbeat. She was so close he was able to still smell the unique fragrance that was hers alone. It did nothing to alleviate his hard-on. If anything, her proximity was just making it worse. All he could think about was pushing her onto her back, pulling her shorts down and sinking into her. He clung to the frayed edges of his self-control like a lifeline.

"I can't go to sleep again now," she complained softly.

"Why not?"

"Because you had your hands down my pants."

Aiden stilled. "I said I was sorry."

"Are you?" She was silent for a moment. "Because I'm not."

Aiden gave an audible groan and would have sat up, but the pressure of her hand on his chest kept him reclined against the pillows. "Lily—"

Leaning over him, she pressed her fingertips against his mouth. "Shh. Don't say anything, Aiden. I know you want this. I felt how much you want this."

He wished he didn't like the sound of his name on her lips so much. She was right—he did want this. He wanted *her.* The dream had been so vivid, and to wake up and find Lily, warm and willing and in his bed was almost more than he could take. But he still had a few functioning brain cells left to tell him that sleeping with Sergeant Lily Munroe was a bad idea.

"Lily," he groaned, at the very edge of restraint, "you don't want this."

In answer, she leaned forward and kissed him, a soft, moist mating of their mouths that made his cock swell and his toes curl. He felt his self-control slip a notch.

"I do," she whispered against his lips. "I've wanted this since the first day I saw you. So unless you're in pain…"

He was in excruciating pain, but not the kind that she thought; the aching in his joints was nothing compared to the aching of his cock. After everything that they'd shared, perhaps she was ready for this. With a groan of defeat, he reached up and buried his hands in her hair. He kissed her with all the pent up desire he'd felt in his dream—that he'd felt for *her* over the past nine months. She made a sound of pleasure in the back of her throat and slid one leg across his hips until she was straddling him, her center pressed against him. She shoved the blankets and duvet cover down to the foot of the bed. The bedroom air was cool, but her body was hot where they touched.

"You feel so good," she breathed. "Please, let me."

"Lily," he gasped, dragging his mouth from hers as she rocked slowly against his erection. "I don't have anything with me—no protection."

"Then we'll improvise."

Before Aiden could guess her intent, she reached between their bodies and cupped him through his shorts. He jerked against her fingers. With a soft hum of approval she stroked him through the fabric.

"Lily," he panted, putting his hand over hers, "what are you doing?"

"Shh," she soothed, and bent forward to press another moist kiss against his mouth. "I want to make you happy. Call it my Christmas gift to you."

"You don't owe me anything," he rasped, as her hand slowly massaged him.

"That's why they call it a gift." Shifting back onto his thighs, she hooked her thumbs in the stretchy waistband of his boxer shorts and slowly eased them down over his straining erection. Aiden lifted his hips to help her, and then he was bare beneath her. His entire body was taut with arousal and anticipation. She was silhouetted above him against the pale backdrop of the canopy, and her thighs pressed against either side of him. "Now the shirt."

She pushed his T-shirt up, and he dragged it over his head and dropped it onto the floor beside the bed. There was something erotic and intensely exciting about the fact that he was naked, while she was still clothed.

Reaching up, he slid a hand beneath the silken fall of her hair and drew her down for a deep kiss, tangling his tongue with hers, making sure she knew he wanted this as much as she did. His free hand pushed beneath her T-shirt to cup her breast. She was soft and firm, and he stroked his thumb over her pebbled nipple. She made a soft gasping sound and reached down to take him in her hand, caressing him and sliding her fingers over his heated flesh.

"You feel amazing," she said against his mouth. "So hard and hot."

Oh, yeah.

She stroked him firmly, smoothing her thumb over the blunted head of his erection and making him groan at the sheer pleasure of it.

"Jesus, Lily," he said through gritted teeth, "you're killing me."

In answer, she lay down beside him, keeping one leg thrown across his thighs as she dragged her mouth from his, and began planting kisses along his jaw and neck. Aiden reached for her, but she surprised him by pushing both hands over his head.

"No touching," she admonished him, but took the sting out of her words by pressing a lingering kiss against his mouth.

It took all Aiden's self-control to just lie there as she kissed and licked her way down his body, especially when she was doing exactly what he had envisioned doing to her. She teased his nipples, flicking them with her tongue. She smoothed her hand over his stomach and hips, and slid her fingers around the base of his straining cock, without ever actually touching him *there*. But when she urged his thighs apart, and gently cupped and kneaded his balls, Aiden's eyes almost rolled back in his head.

"Feel good?" she asked. Finally, she wrapped her fingers around him, squeezing and stroking him. And when she dipped her head and ran her tongue along his length, Aiden couldn't prevent his guttural sound of pleasure.

Lily made a humming sound of approval, and took him in her mouth. There was nothing shy or hesitant about her style; she clearly knew what she was doing and delighted in driving him wild. Aiden's toes curled. The hot, wet sensation of her lips and tongue on his shaft was almost more than he could take, but when she squeezed the base with her fingers and simultaneously cupped his balls, he thought he might actually die.

He groaned loudly, and reached down to stroke her hair. She increased her tempo, drawing him deeply into her mouth and swirling her tongue over him as she released him. The rhythmic movement of her hand in concert with her mouth was his undoing.

"Lily," he managed, his voice hoarse, "I'm about six seconds away from losing it."

"I know," she said, and angled her head to look at him. "I want it all."

Her response was so unexpected, and so incredibly arousing, that it only took two more sweeps of her tongue to undo him. He came in a blinding rush of white-hot pleasure, gritting his teeth against the exquisite explosion of release. He lay there, completely drained.

Lily crawled up beside him and he pulled her against his chest.

"I wasn't expecting that," he said gruffly.

He felt her smile against his shoulder. "I know. Those are the best kind of gifts."

He tipped her face up and kissed her. He was still a little weak from the force of his release, but he wasn't ready to roll over and go to sleep. Not by a long shot.

Twisting, he pulled Lily beneath him. "Now it's your turn," he promised.

She tried to demur, but he felt her squirm a little beneath him. "You don't have to do anything," she said. "This isn't something where I expect you to reciprocate."

"I know," he said, pressing a kiss against the corner of her mouth. "But I've dreamed of doing this for a long time now, so if you think you're getting away that easily, you're wrong."

"Oh." She laughed. "Well, in that case, I wouldn't dream of trying to escape."

"It wouldn't do you any good," Aiden assured her, smiling.

Then there were no more words as he kissed her. Reaching beneath her shirt, he fondled her breasts, cupping and squeezing them until she arched into his palm. Shoving the fabric up, he dipped his head, licking and suckling each breast in turn. He smoothed his hand over her ribs and stomach, until he reached the juncture of her thighs. Pushing his hand into her shorts, he cupped her beneath the slippery fabric of her panties.

"God, I want to see you down here," he muttered against her breast. "Turn on a light."

Lily laughed uncertainly, and then stopped. "Wait. Are you serious?"

"You bet," he said. He reached past her and switched on the tiny bedside lamp. Gazing at Lily, he saw her face was flushed with arousal, and what might have been embarrassment. Her normally sleek hair was tousled, and her mouth was swollen from kissing him. The expression in her dark eyes was actually a little shy. Aiden thought she'd never been more beautiful. "Man, you are gorgeous."

"No, I'm not." She actually blushed, and dropped her eyes from his.

"Then you haven't looked into a mirror lately," Aiden said drily. "You're stunning." Grasping the edge of her T-shirt, he pulled it up and over her head. Her breasts were full and firm, and tipped with the most perfect pink nipples he'd ever seen. "And you're hot," he added, covering her with both hands.

Lily gave a gurgle of laughter that quickly turned to a moan of pleasure as Aiden lifted and squeezed her pliant flesh, teasing the pebbled tips with his tongue and teeth. As he slowly worked his way down her body, kissing and licking and biting, she put her hands on his head, caressing his ears and the nape of his neck, and rubbing her fingers over his short hair. Her touch spurred him on, and so when he reached the edge of her shorts, he didn't hesitate, but quickly pushed them down over her thighs, taking her panties with them and watching as she kicked them free.

He reared back to stare at her. Her body was slim and pale, except for her lush breasts, which were rosy from his attention. And at the apex of her thighs, she had just a narrow strip of dark hair, but was otherwise bare. Aiden found himself growing hard again just looking at her.

"Open for me," he commanded in a husky voice, and nudged her legs apart with his hands. "Oh, man, you are gorgeous down here, too, all pink and soft."

He stroked a finger along one side of her outer lips, and she shivered. She made a small sound of pleasure. Watching the tension on her face, he tormented her a little, caressing her everywhere but where she most needed it.

"If you don't touch me soon," she gasped, "I'm going to die."

"I'm going to do more than just touch you," he promised, stroking a single finger along her center, parting her. "Oh, baby, you're so wet."

"That's what you do to me," she panted, pushing herself up on her elbows to watch him.

Aiden swirled her moisture around, slicking it over the small rise of flesh so that she gave a small whimper of pleasure.

"Do you like that?" he asked, rubbing his thumb against her.

"I'm not sure how long I'm going to last," she said in a ragged voice. "I'm already so close."

Her words caused lust to jackknife through him, and he eased himself down on the mattress. Pushing her thighs apart, he bent his head and licked her once along the seam of her sex. She tasted light and delicate, and he pressed his tongue softly against her clitoris, before sucking the small nub into his mouth. She cried out, and then her hands were in his hair, rubbing his scalp and caressing his ears, urging him on. Aiden had dreamed of doing this to her, but the reality was so much better than anything he could have imagined. The small noises she made as he licked and stroked her only ratcheted up his own desire.

Pulling back, he rubbed his fingers over her as he watched her face, tight with concentration. He eased one finger into her, and her mouth formed a soundless *O* of pleasure. She was incredibly snug and hot, and as he worked a second finger into her, he bent his head and flicked her hard with his tongue. Her inner muscles clenched around him, and he wanted badly to replace his fingers with his cock; to drive into her and cause her to cry out in mindless release.

"Oh, I'm so close," she panted. Her eyes were hazy as she gripped his arms and tried to urge him upward. "Come inside me."

Aiden lifted his head, telling himself to slow down. Clearly, she was no longer in control, so it was up to him to maintain some sense of reason. "Baby," he rasped, "I'd love to do that, but we don't have any protection."

"I'm on the Pill," she said urgently. "And I'm completely clean. I know you are, too."

"Lily, I'm not sure—"

"I am. Please, Aiden, come inside me. I need you inside me!"

Her words caused him to lose the tenuous grip he had on his own self-control, feeling it slip through his fingers like water. He ached to join himself with her. "Lily—"

"*Please,* Aiden!"

With a low growl of need, he threw caution aside and released her, positioning himself at her entrance. She was slippery and hot, and he surged into her with one powerful thrust. She gasped, and then she was riding him hard, her legs hooked around his thighs, her hands clutching his shoulders. She gripped him strongly, and Aiden pumped himself into her, feeling her inner muscles fist around him. When her orgasm hit her, she gasped his name, and the sound was enough to catapult him over the edge with her, in a mind-blowing burst of ecstasy.

For long moments, there was only the sound of their uneven breathing. Lily stroked his back in lazy sweeps of her fingertips. He was probably crushing her, but he lacked the strength to move.

"Hey," Lily murmured in his ear. "Are you okay?"

He nodded, and with a groan he pushed himself to one side, pulling her with him. "That was completely reckless—you do get that?"

In answer, she wound her arms around him and kissed his jaw. "We're fine," she assured him. "I'm safe, and I know you are, too. I've seen your medical record."

Aiden gave a huff of disbelieving laughter, but there was a part of him that admired her practicality. "Well, okay." He pulled back enough to search her eyes. "No regrets?"

"Are you kidding me? I already told you—I've wanted this since the first day I saw you. What about you? Do you regret it?"

Aiden shook his head. "Never."

Reaching down, he dragged the blankets over them, and then snapped off the light. He lay there, with Lily's warm body pressed against him, surrounded by her scent and listening to the sound of her breathing. He had absolutely no regrets. He couldn't imagine he'd ever be sorry that he'd made love to Lily Munroe. He'd told her that he didn't do one-night stands, so he had to believe that she'd had a change of heart; that she was willing to give them a shot at a real relationship. He hoped so, because right now, he felt like it was his birthday and Christmas all at once.

6

WHEN LILY WOKE UP in the morning, she was alone. The room was empty, but someone had lit a fire in the fireplace, taking the chill away. Dragging the blankets with her, she rolled onto her side, and found a note tucked under the pillow beside her head. Smiling, she unfolded it. "Didn't want to wake you. Come downstairs when you're ready. –A.C."

Not exactly romantic, but Aiden had never struck her as a particularly romantic man. Oddly enough, it was partly what had attracted her to him. There was something incredibly sexy about a guy who focused so completely on his work, especially when that work was so dangerous. It had made her wonder what it would be like to have all that intensity focused on her.

Now she knew.

She could still feel his hands and mouth on her, and her body was deliciously tender in unexpected places. She tried to recall how long it had been since she'd last had sex, and failed. Her last relationship—if you could even call it that—had ended almost a year ago, when she had been deployed to Africa. She'd been more relieved than disappointed about the breakup and hadn't really been interested in anyone since—until Aiden. Closing his note in her palm, she wondered why he hadn't stuck around for a repeat performance this morning—unless maybe he was having some regrets, after all.

But she'd all but told him that she didn't do commitment, so perhaps he'd found a way to accept that this time might be all they had and had decided to take advantage of it.

Glancing at the bedside clock, she saw with alarm that it was almost nine o'clock. With a groan, she sat up and pushed the covers aside, shivering a little as the cooler air touched her naked skin. She'd take a shower and then go downstairs to find out when they would leave for Fort Atterbury. And hope that things wouldn't be too awkward between her and Aiden.

Thirty minutes later, as she made her way down the winding staircase, she could hear the sound of excited voices, and smell the delicious aroma of cinnamon. For a moment, it brought her back to her early childhood, when her mother was still well enough to bake muffins in the morning, and Lily would sit on the kitchen counter and help her.

Pushing the memories aside, she made her way through the house. The pretty dining room was empty except for Inge's daughter, Abby, who was organizing flatware at a long sidebar. She glanced up and smiled at Lily.

"Good morning. Your boyfriend is in the kitchen with the kids." Her smile widened. "They're pretty taken with him."

With an uncertain murmur of thanks, Lily continued on to the kitchen. Despite the coziness of the living room, with its large fireplace and comfortable sofas, this was clearly the heart of the house. An enormous island dominated the room. Beyond that, situated in front of a bank of French doors overlooking the backyard, stood a long farm table.

For a moment, Lily just stood in the doorway and watched. Aiden stood at the stove, wearing a bright red apron over his fatigues and a Santa hat. Perched on stools beside him were two children; a little girl who looked to be about four or five, and the little boy they'd met the previous night. Aiden was making pancakes, and the children were judging how well he poured the batter into the shapes they demanded. Two older girls sat at the farm table eating pancakes smothered in strawberries and heaped high with whipped cream.

Nearby, Inge was in the process of taking two cookie sheets out of a double wall oven. As she turned to place the hot sheets onto the cooling racks, she spotted Lily in the doorway.

"Ah, there you are," she called cheerfully. "Just in time, too. I hope you're hungry, because we have enough pancakes to feed—well, an army! There's a fruit platter on the table, and I have a plate of sausages warming in the lower oven."

Aiden met her gaze, and the warm welcome in his eyes dispelled all her worries. "Hey," he said, his eyes sweeping over her. "Sleep well?"

She came over to the stove to watch him expertly flip a pancake. "Yes. Why didn't you wake me?"

"You were out like a light, and I didn't have the heart to disturb you." He slanted her a sidelong look and lowered his voice. "Besides, after last night, you needed your sleep."

Lily shot a glance at the children, but they were engrossed in carrying their plates of pancakes over to the table. She felt herself go warm beneath his steady regard and cleared her throat uncomfortably.

"About last night—" She broke off, unsure how to continue.

Setting the spatula aside, he stepped close to her. Using one finger, he tucked a strand of hair behind her ear. "I'm just glad you changed your mind."

Lily frowned. "What do you mean?"

He stroked a thumb along her jaw. "You've decided to take a chance on a real relationship. I'm glad."

Lily bit her lip, unsure what to say. She'd thought he'd understood that their time together wouldn't extend beyond Gingerbread Cottage. How could it? Once they returned to California, they'd have little opportunity to see each other. That Aiden believed they had any chance at a future together panicked her. She wouldn't live up to his expectations, or be the kind of woman that he wanted—the kind of woman he deserved.

Thankfully she was saved from having to answer when Inge came over to the stove to check on his progress.

"So what is it you're doing, Santa?" Lily asked brightly, changing the subject.

"I am helping Sarah and Josh make pancakes in the shape of reindeer. See?" He indicated the frying pan. "Here is the reindeer, and these are the antlers."

Lily tipped her head and considered them. "They're spotted reindeer."

The girl, Sarah, giggled from the table. "Those are chocolate chips."

"Ah." Lily gave Aiden an admiring glance. "They're actually very realistic."

Aiden chuckled. "Years of practice, making pancakes at home."

He grew silent as he flipped the pancakes onto a waiting plate, and Lily knew he was thinking of his family.

"Did you call Ann?" she ventured quietly. "What time should we be at the base?"

His lips compressed, and he shook his head. "We're not going anywhere today. They're completely jammed up, and Ann said they're having trouble booking flights out of Indianapolis or Cincinnati, partly because of the strong winds and partly because most of them are already full." He turned his gaze toward her. "We may not get a flight out until after Christmas."

Lily watched him, sensing his disappointment and frustration. Before she could say anything, he scooped the remaining pancakes onto a plate and indicated the table.

"C'mon, let's eat."

Lily followed him to the table and sat down across from

two teenaged girls, who stared openly at Aiden, and then giggled in delight when he gave them a cheeky wink. Lily couldn't blame them; he looked irresistible in his apron and hat. If Santa really looked like him, she'd never go to bed on Christmas Eve.

"These are my older granddaughters, Emma and Sophia," said Inge as she poured coffee for Aiden and Lily, and set a plate of breakfast sausages in front of them. "I offered to bring you breakfast in your room, or in the dining room, but your young man said he preferred the kitchen. Said it reminded him of home."

Lily smiled. "This is wonderful. Thank you so much for letting us intrude on your family holiday."

Inge waved away her thanks. "You're not intruding, and it's Christmas, after all." She put her hand on Lily's shoulder. "I'm honored to have you here, and although I'm not your mother, I'd like to treat you both as if you were my own, for the sake of every mother who won't be spending Christmas with her son or daughter this season."

Lily fell silent as Aiden murmured his thanks. When Inge stepped away, he reached out and covered her hand with his beneath the lace tablecloth, squeezing her fingers, and Lily felt the aching tightness in her chest ease.

Then Aiden tucked into his breakfast with an appetite that she hadn't seen since before his illness.

"How are you feeling this morning?" she asked quietly as she speared a wedge of melon.

"Great," he assured her. "Never better."

His hand still encased hers, and she threw a quick glance at the children, but they were engrossed in eating. She kept her voice low.

"So, last night—"

He angled his head and looked at her, waiting.

But Lily's nerve slipped a little beneath the intensity of

those blue eyes. He raised one eyebrow, as if he were challenging her in some way.

"Nothing," she finally said, and dropped her attention to her plate.

Aiden leaned over until his lips were against her ear. "Last night," he whispered, "was amazing."

Straightening, he ate a forkful of pancakes without taking his eyes off her, and then gave her a wink. Across the table, the older girls giggled again.

Lily waited until the children were too busy eating and talking to pay attention, and then pressed close to Aiden. "Last night *was* amazing," she agreed in a whisper. "But it was just one night, Aiden. I never agreed to something more."

Aiden didn't look at her, but he was listening. She felt him tense, and a muscle worked in his lean jaw.

"We can talk about this later," he finally said.

"No, I need you to understand. I don't want to give you the wrong idea."

This time, he did look at her, and the expression in his blue eyes was so tender that Lily felt her chest constrict.

"I understand more than you know," he finally said, reaching out to squeeze her hand. "Just trust me. Everything is going to be fine."

Lily drew in a deep breath, overwhelmed by his confidence and easy assurance.

"We have a busy day planned," Inge said, pulling ingredients out of the cupboards and setting them on the center island. "I hope you'll join us."

"We should call Ann again," Lily said, before Aiden could respond. "Just to be sure. What if they're making good progress?"

Inge paused and gave her a sympathetic look. "I'm sorry, my dear. I talked with Ann this morning, too, and she said that they're making arrangements for the soldiers to spend

Christmas at Fort Atterbury. There's just no way to get them all processed and home in time for the holiday."

Lily digested the news in silence. She and Aiden would spend Christmas together at Gingerbread Cottage. She kept her expression carefully neutral. She had no right to feel so elated, not when Aiden had been so looking forward to getting home, and not when he would misinterpret their time together.

"So you see," Inge said. "It's all settled. The men should be back any moment now."

Lily stared at Inge in surprise. "Men?"

"My husband and my two boys." She laughed as she measured out several cups of flour and dumped them into a mixing bowl. "Of course, they're grown men, now, but they always spend Christmas Eve here at Gingerbread Cottage. They went out to get a tree."

Lily's eyebrows shot up. She thought her father was the only person who waited until the day before Christmas to get a tree, and that was usually because she guilted him into doing it. Most people she knew got their tree the day after Thanksgiving.

"We have a tradition of putting our tree up on Christmas Eve," Inge explained, correctly interpreting Lily's expression. "The men go to a small tree farm about three miles down the road where they cut a tree and bring it back."

"And tonight we'll decorate it," Sarah piped in. "I always put the star on the top. It's tradition."

Lily suspected this family had a lot of traditions. "That sounds wonderful. Will you let me help with the decorations?"

"Of course," said the oldest girl, Emma. "We also do lots of baking in the afternoon."

Aiden frowned. "So there's decorating and baking. What do the men do?"

"Drink," the children chimed together, and Aiden laughed.

"Then we go to Christmas Eve service," Sophie chirped. "We hold candles and sing songs."

"When we get home, we eat and then we get ready for Santa Claus," Josh said solemnly. "We have to be in bed by nine o'clock."

"I like that plan," Aiden said. "In fact, Lily and I will probably be in bed at nine o'clock, too, just to make sure we don't ruin Santa's plans." Beneath the table, Lily kicked him, and he gave her a wide-eyed look of innocence. "What?"

"That will be the men now," Inge said, wiping her hands on her apron as she peered through the windows. The children hurried to the windows, wiping the condensation aside with their fingers in order to peer outside.

Lily heard the rumble of an engine, and a pickup truck pulled into the driveway near the back door.

"I see them," Sophie exclaimed excitedly. "They have a tree!"

As Aiden and Lily watched, the back door opened, and three men entered amidst a gust of bitter cold air. All three of them wore heavy winter parkas, paired with big boots, which they stomped enthusiastically on the rug. Inge fluttered around them, scolding them for tracking ice onto her floor.

"I'd have stripped down outside," the oldest man said, reaching out to pinch Sophie's cheek, "but I was afraid of turning into a big Popsicle."

"This is my husband, Peter," said Inge to Aiden. "And these two giants are my sons, Garth and Seth."

"Did you get a good tree, Uncle Garth?" Sarah asked, bouncing up and down beside the men.

"The best," Garth assured her. "Plenty of room for decorations."

"And for presents underneath," teased Seth, swinging the little girl up into his arms and pressing his cold face against her cheeks and neck, as she squealed in delight.

Setting the child on her feet, he took a plate from the counter and nodded a greeting as he sat down across from Lily and Aiden, snagging a sausage with his fingers.

"Welcome to Gingerbread Cottage," Peter said, coming over to shake their hands. "And thank you for what you do in defense of our country." He indicated his older son. "Garth served with the U.S. Marines for eight years after he graduated college."

"I'm in the navy, and Sergeant Munroe is in the army," Aiden said.

"Please call me Lily," she said, shifting uncomfortably beneath their scrutiny.

"Where are you coming from?" Seth asked as he speared a fork through several pancakes and loaded them onto his plate.

"Africa," Aiden said, but didn't give any additional information.

The men nodded as if they understood his reticence. "Quite the difference in climate," Peter offered. "I hope you have some warm outer gear with you."

"We each have a sweater and a jacket," Lily said. "But not anything sufficient for this cold."

"We usually go sledding today," Emma chimed in from the table. "It's tradition."

"We'll have to deviate from tradition this year," her grandfather said. "It's below zero outside, so I don't think sledding would be any fun today."

The children groaned in disappointment.

"You know," Aiden began, "my family has a Christmas tradition that you might like to adopt." Four faces turned expectantly toward him. "Where I come from, there's no snow, so we make our own."

"How do you do that?" Sarah demanded, scrunching up her nose.

"If you have some white paper and a pair of scissors, I'll show you," he offered.

The kids quickly vanished in search of the items, returning armed with a thick stack of copier paper and a plastic fishing tackle box that was filled with scissors, tape and colored pencils.

"Okay, we're ready," Emma said.

Aiden exchanged a grin with Lily, before dramatically stretching his arms and flexing his fingers, like a magician about to perform a trick. "Okay," he said, "prepare to be amazed."

The children crowded around him, kneeling on their chairs with their elbows on the table for a better view. The adults, including Lily, came to stand around the table and watched as Aiden deftly folded a single sheet of paper over and then over, and over again. When he was finished, he passed it around to the children to show them how he had folded it into a narrow triangle, explaining why it was important to fold it just so. Then, picking up a pair of scissors, he began snipping away at the edges of the paper.

"And now," he said, carefully unfolding the paper, "you have your snowflake."

As he flattened the paper out, Lily saw he had created a beautiful, lacy snowflake. The younger children exclaimed their delight, and began snatching sheets of paper and started folding them.

Aiden was infinitely patient as he showed each child in turn how to fold the paper, and where to cut to create the best patterns. As Lily watched, her heart swelled with affection for this man who could be so tough, and yet so tender.

"That's quite a man you have there," Inge said softly, as she stood beside Lily. "I'd say he's a keeper."

Lily nodded. He was a keeper. She'd suspected as much from the beginning, but now she knew it was the truth. Only he'd never be hers to keep. They wanted different things, and as much as she might want Aiden, she wasn't what he needed. As if sensing her emotions were close to the surface, Inge turned to the men.

"Why don't you bring the tree onto the porch, and set it in the stand. We'll let it dry off and open a bit before we bring it into the parlor."

"Can I help?" Lily asked, feeling as if she should be doing something.

Josh raised his head and looked at her. "Do you have any traditions? Now we have Aiden's tradition of paper snow-flakes added to our day. What about you?"

Aiden's eyes met hers, his hands pausing in their work.

Lily flushed. "Well, to be honest, we didn't do much to celebrate Christmas when I was little." Seeing their puzzled faces, she hastened to explain. "My mother was very sick, and my father spent most of his time taking care of her."

Josh appeared bewildered. "But didn't you have *any* traditions?"

"Josh—" Inge began to silence the child, but Lily stopped her.

"No, it's okay. One year, I spent Christmas with my grandparents, and there was something they liked to do that I guess could be called a tradition," she offered. She looked at Aiden and saw something in his eyes that might have been a combination of compassion and pride, and something else that she didn't dare name, but which gave her courage. She glanced back at the children and smiled. "We made a batch of magic oats for Santa's reindeer before we put together a plate of cookies for Santa."

"Everyone puts out cookies for Santa," Josh scoffed.

"Josh, hush," scolded Emma. To Lily, she said, "Making magic oats sounds great. That's something we've never done."

"You could help us," Sophie added. "It will be our new

tradition. And maybe you and Aiden will feel like you're at home for Christmas, and not with strangers."

Lily wanted to give the girl a hug. Sophie didn't realize that this was quickly becoming the most memorable Christmas Lily had ever had. She gave the little girl a wide smile.

"We can make the magic oats after you've finished making snowflakes," she promised. "And you know what? I already don't think of you as strangers." Her voice broke a little bit, and she cleared her throat, hoping nobody noticed.

This was the kind of family that she had longed for as a little girl; the kind of Christmas that she had dreamed of. This is what Aiden was promising to give to the woman who could commit to a life with him. But the thought of giving herself over to someone so completely made her breathless and panicky.

As if sensing her inner agitation, Inge put an arm around her shoulders and squeezed. "This Christmas," she announced, "Aiden and Lily are part of our family."

"Thank you," Lily murmured. "You don't know how much that means to me."

Inge seemed touched, and a little embarrassed. "Well, I mean every word of it. Of course," she warned, "being part of the Buchwald family means you also get to share in the preparation of dinner, as well as the baskets we bring to the church for charity. And then there's the tree to decorate and games to play, before we can even think about Santa. Are you ready?"

Lily smiled and her gaze shifted to Aiden. "Yes, I think I am."

7

BY THE TIME the children were nestled, all snug in their beds, it was nearly ten o'clock. Little Sarah was so sleepy that her father had to carry her up the stairs, while Seth lifted Josh onto his shoulders, much to the little boy's delight.

"They're excited and overtired," observed Inge, "but they'll be asleep as soon as their heads hit the pillow. Happens every year."

"You have a wonderful family," Lily said, setting her mug of hot chocolate down on the coffee table.

They'd had a long and busy day, and while there was a part of Lily that was reluctant to see it end, there was another part of her that couldn't wait to be alone with Aiden. She needed to know if she was only imagining the closeness and sense of intimacy that had been building between them all day. She wasn't so naive as to believe that just because they had slept together, they would stay together. But did she *want* them to stay together? Before she'd met Aiden, she couldn't imagine herself even wanting something permanent. But right now…she wasn't sure. All she was sure of was that she needed to feel his arms around her, to be reassured that last night hadn't been a dream. She'd been aware of Aiden watching her when he thought she wasn't looking, until she felt as if her stretched nerves would snap. What was he thinking? How did he feel about her? She had to know.

Even the church service, as lovely as it had been, had only served to increase her growing sexual frustration. She had sat next to Aiden, his hard thigh pressed against hers, his fingers just brushing her own. She could smell him—an intoxicating blend of clean soap and musky male that made it nearly impossible to think about anything except sex. They'd driven to the church in Peter's four-wheel drive, but Lily had been forced to sit on Aiden's lap. His hand had slid inside her jacket to rest on her hip, and she'd been all too aware of the effect she was having on him.

Now they sat together in the living room, the tree freshly decorated, while a fire snapped and crackled in the fireplace. Aiden had spoken with Ann several more times during the day, and she'd told them it would take at least another day to get through the backlog. They wouldn't be getting home in time for Christmas.

Aiden occupied one side of the sofa, and Lily was curled up beside him, her stockinged feet tucked beneath her. She allowed herself to lean against his hard shoulder, without actually snuggling.

"Well," Inge said, as she rose to her feet with a sly smile, "I think it's time we went to bed, but you kids stay up for as long as you like. We'll see you in the morning."

"Oh, please," Lily protested to Inge's retreating back. "Don't go on our account. In fact, we're heading upstairs ourselves."

But Inge had disappeared, and as Peter rose to his feet to follow her, he shrugged and smiled. "There's no use arguing with the woman. She always gets her way, I can promise you that. Good night."

Garth threw another log onto the fire. "Dad's right," he said, and stretched dramatically. "There's no point in arguing with my mother. But the fact is, I'm bushed. See you in the morning."

Lily found herself alone with Aiden. "Okay, why do I have the distinct feeling this was all planned?"

Aiden rose to his feet and crossed the room to where a laptop sat on a side table. "Because it was. Although, in my own defense, I never asked them to leave. I simply told them there was something I wanted to give you tonight, after the kids were in bed."

"What is it?" Lily asked, uncurling herself and sitting up straight. Anxiety washed over her. "I hope you didn't get me a gift, because I don't have anything to give you in return."

Aiden grinned at her. "Yeah, you do."

Carrying the laptop over to the sofa, he switched it on and began working the keyboard. "I hope you don't mind, but I wanted to give you a Christmas with you father."

"Skype," Lily breathed, watching the picture come up on the screen. She had used Skype before, but only with friends, never with her father. She didn't even know he owned a computer. Reaching out blindly, she gripped Aiden's knee. He shifted closer. "I'm right here."

As he finished setting up the connection, her father's face suddenly appeared on the small screen.

"Dad," Lily exclaimed. "Can you hear me?"

Her father appeared older than she remembered, but the expression of sadness that seemed as much a part of him as his green work shirts was absent. He actually looked… happy.

"Hello, Lily Bell," he said, and smiled.

Lily Bell. She'd almost forgotten the childhood nickname that he used to call her.

"Hey, Dad, you look good."

"So do you. Thin, but good. Are you okay?"

She nodded. "Yes, I'm fine. I'm sorry I can't be there." She swallowed hard, his warm expression dredging up old emotions, so that she suddenly feared she might cry. "I miss you, Dad."

"I miss you, too, Lily Bell. Who is that with you?"

"Hello, sir," Aiden said. "We spoke earlier. I'm Chief Cross. I traveled with Lily from Africa. She saved my life in the jungle."

Lily gave him a halfhearted shove. "I did not. You would have recovered without me."

"I'm glad you're with her, son," her father said. "I hate to think of my Lily spending Christmas alone." He paused. "She's spent too many holidays alone."

"Dad, don't." Lily didn't want to bring up the past, didn't want Aiden or any of the Buchwalds feeling sorry for her.

"It's okay, sir," Aiden was saying. "I intend for her not to spend any more holidays alone if I can help it."

Lily stared at him, astonished, but he simply arched an eyebrow at her, as if daring her to contradict him. She glanced away, focusing instead on the laptop, aware that her heart was beating fast. Her father was talking to someone offscreen, and Lily realized she recognized his surroundings and it wasn't his home.

"Dad, are you at the diner?" She couldn't keep the disbelief out of her voice.

He had the grace to look sheepish. "They're having a little Christmas Eve gathering, and I figured it would be nice not to spend the night by myself."

Lily gaped at him. "Dad, that's wonderful! I'm so glad you're not at the house, alone."

"There's actually someone I wanted you to meet while you were home, Lily, but now is as good a time as any." He looked away from the camera and gestured to someone that Lily couldn't see. In the next instant, a woman's face appeared. She was an attractive older woman, and Lily recognized her as a waitress at the diner. "This is Pamela. We've been dating for about a year now."

For a moment, Lily was too stunned to speak. Her father—dating? But suddenly, it all made sense. All the meals he ate at the diner; why he was never at home when she called. She wouldn't be surprised if he was actually living with Pamela.

"It's great to meet you," she said now. "I hope I'll be able to get home in the next day or so, and you and I can meet in person."

"I'd like that," Pamela said.

They chatted for a few more minutes before wishing each other Merry Christmas, and then they ended the connection. For a moment, Lily just sat there, trying to take it all in. Her father, it seemed, had finally moved on. He appeared to be happy, and the knowledge made her happy, too. More than that, she felt hopeful, both for her father and for herself—if he could give his heart again, then maybe she could, too. Slowly, she became aware that Aiden was gently rubbing her back.

"So that was my dad," she said, still in disbelief. "Or at least someone who looked a lot like him."

"Nice guy."

"Yeah. He sure seemed happy."

"So now you can relax and enjoy Christmas. Your dad is okay, and you don't have to feel guilty about not being home with him."

She stared at him. "How did you know?"

"Know what?" He gave her a wide-eyed look of innocence.

"How I was feeling? About Christmas? About being home?"

Aiden closed the laptop and turned toward her on the sofa, covering her hands with his own. "Listen, I realize I freaked you out with my talk about a long-term relationship. But I meant what I said. I want to give us a shot at something real. Because what we have is pretty amazing."

Lily stared down at their hands without answering. What they had *was* amazing, but there was still a part of her that went into full panic mode at the thought of committing herself to just one person.

"Lily," he said earnestly, dipping his head to look directly into her eyes. "I get that I'm putting a lot of pressure on you, and I'm sorry. But I wanted you to know that for me, this is serious. But I'm willing to give you all the time you need to get used to the idea, okay?"

His eyes were bluer than she had ever seen them. "Really?"

"Really." He gave her a lopsided grin. "All relationships start somewhere. We'll just take it a day at a time. And if I have to come up to Crescent City every weekend to convince you of my feelings, I'll do it."

Lily returned his smile. "Or I could find a job in your area, once your mission in Africa is over."

"Yeah," he said softly. "That would work, too."

Before she could protest, he leaned forward and pressed a kiss against her mouth, and Lily felt her body respond to the implicit promise in that kiss. Too soon, he pulled away so that he could gaze directly into her eyes.

"I've been dying to kiss you. It's been the only thing on my mind all day. How about we call it a night and go to bed?"

Lily's first impulse was to grab his hand and drag him upstairs, but still she hesitated. "Don't you want to Skype with your family?"

"No, it's okay, I talked with them earlier. Maybe we can set something up for tomorrow, after the kids have opened their presents. They're dying to meet you."

She looked at him suspiciously. "They are? Why?"

"I told them that you cared for me in Africa."

Not just in Africa. She cared for him *now*. More than she wanted to admit, even to herself. What had started out as simple attraction had slowly become so much more. She'd had the chance to get to know Aiden Cross, and everything about the man appealed to her.

"I did," she murmured. "I do."

Standing, he tugged her to her feet and headed for the staircase, pulling her behind him. Lily gave an uncertain laugh, even as anticipation surged through her. She let him pull her up the stairs and along the corridor to their room. As soon as he closed the door, he turned and hauled her into his arms. Tipping her face up, he kissed her deeply, and so sweetly that something within Lily shifted and broke loose in her chest.

"Lily Munroe," he said, all humor gone. "I've been wanting to get you alone all day."

Lily searched his eyes, feeling a little weak at the expression she saw reflected there. "I woke up and you weren't there. I wondered—" She broke off.

He cupped her face, a warm smile curving his mouth. "What did you wonder, sweetheart?"

"If maybe you regretted what happened last night."

Aiden laughed softly. "Oh, baby, you have no idea how much I wanted last night to happen. I wanted you the first time I saw you in Entebbe."

"I'm sorry I led you to believe I was interested in your friend." She flushed. "I'm ashamed to admit that I was just trying to get a reaction out of you."

He bent his head to hers. "Let's forget all that. We're here now, and that's all that matters. It's Christmas Eve, and I can't imagine anyone I'd rather share the holiday with."

"Oh, Aiden…"

Releasing her, he crossed the room to where he'd left his backpack on one of the chairs. Someone had lit a fire in the fireplace and left a plate of cookies on the small table by the chairs. Opening the backpack, Aiden pulled out a small bag. "In fact, I have something for you."

Lily frowned. "For me?"

He smiled and caught her hand, pulling her toward him. Lowering himself into the empty chair, he pulled her down onto his lap. She leaned against him and watched as he opened the bag and withdrew a small packet, wrapped in tissue paper.

"I found this in Entebbe. I haven't had a chance to wrap it," he apologized, "but when I saw this, I knew you had to have it."

Mystified, Lily took the packet from him. Closing her fingers around it, she looked at him. "I don't have anything for you."

Pulling her face down, Aiden pressed a warm kiss against her mouth. "You've already given me more than I ever dreamed of. Go ahead. Open it."

Carefully, Lily unfolded the delicate tissue and stared at what lay inside. It was beautiful pendant necklace, an intricately wrought, multifingered silver star that might have been a snowflake. Speechless, she lifted the necklace in her fingers.

"It's the most beautiful thing anyone has ever given me," she said, her voice breaking a little.

"It's called the Star of Africa, and it reminded me of a snowflake. You were always complaining about the jungle heat, so I thought you'd appreciate this," he said. "Here, let me help you put it on."

Taking the necklace from her, he put it around her neck, his fingers brushing her skin as he fastened it. She smoothed her fingers over the star, admiring how the cut silver caught the light and reflected it back. Aiden stroked his knuckles along her jaw and down the side of her neck, until he lifted the star in his fingers.

"It suits you, but I think it would look better against your bare skin."

Turning to him, she pressed a soft, moist kiss against

his mouth. "I'm not sure…you're still recovering. I don't want to strain you."

Aiden made a sound that was half laugh and half growl, and bent her over his arm, one hand sliding beneath the hem of her shirt to smooth over her torso. Lily reveled in the feel of his fingers against her bare skin.

"I'm already strained," he rasped against her mouth. "I'm hoping you can relieve that strain."

Lily gave a soft hum of approval and wound her arms around his neck. "It *is* Christmas…"

Aiden pulled back and searched her eyes. "You're not sorry that you're stuck here with me, are you?"

Lily stared at him. "Are you kidding? This is hands down the best Christmas I've ever had. Seriously." She paused. "What about you, though? You were really looking forward to going home."

His expression was so incredibly tender, Lily's heart quickened.

"Lily," he said softy, "don't you know? Being here with you—like this—is something I only ever dreamed about. With you, I feel like I *am* home."

"Oh, Aiden," she breathed, too overwhelmed to express the many emotions she was experiencing. "I meant what I said—this is the most wonderful Christmas I've ever had. You've made all of my wishes come true."

"Well, not all of them," he said, and stood up, lifting her in his arms. He strode to the bed and laid her down on top of it, stretching out beside her and gathering her into his arms. "But I intend to, starting right now."

"Oh, Aiden…"

* * * * *